Galloping Across a Cornish Summer

by Cate Bryant

© September, 2017

Cover Photograph kindly supplied by Sandra Roberts

Table of Contents

Chapter One

Fred, the old dun pony was neighing down the valley and woke Jenny, who was huddled into her threadbare duvet on the top bunk while her sister, Amanda slept undisturbed below her. There had been five wonderful horses with seahorse heads galloping through her dream but they vanished into the ethereal cold of the unheated council house as she opened her eyes. She tried to catch hold of the edge of her dream that had been full of the certainty of happiness, but all she could remember was an impression of shimmering bright green grass on a sunlit meadow. Now she could hear nothing but the desolate cry of a crow, and then the sound of a motorbike starting up next door.

There was an ache inside Jenny that nothing but horses would assuage. They were in her thoughts by day, and in her dreams by night. Her yearning for ponies was like an unquenchable thirst. Fred was a new arrival in the neighbourhood, living in a field up the stream that ran past Jenny's back garden. It was common knowledge in the village that the pony had been leased from the Penzance Riding School by the woman from London who was renting the property. Nobody knew anything about the woman and so far, she had not been seen in the village.

From Jenny's back door, she could run up the stream to Fred's field in just ten minutes. She had been visiting him every morning before school, taking sliced carrots and stolen lumps of sugar. Fred was always pleased to see her, lonely without any other horses he was happy to have some company. Jenny had rather hoped that the woman in the house might appear and offer to let her ride him, but so far there had been no sign of her.

She jumped down lightly onto the floor, careful not to disturb her sister. Pulling on an old coat that served as a dressing gown and she ran to the window and looked out across the untidy back garden choked with rank grass and weeds. But there was nothing to see in the grey swirling mist; certainly no horses in sight. Fred was upstream, but in her dream there had been more than just him. The five imaginary horses had been divine, silky coated, well-bred and

3

magical. But the feeling persisted, as if her dream had been more real than her everyday life.

She decided to run up and check on Fred, just in case. It was only six-thirty, no one in the household would be stirring until eight when there would be a general relentless struggle as the family of five children, roused by their weary mother got up, shrugged themselves into clothes and stumbled out the front door to get to school more or less on time. Jenny dressed in her old jeans and favourite faded blue denim jacket and crept down the worn, dirty, carpeted stairs to the back door. It took only half a minute to cross the garden and slip through the broken fence onto the broad stream path that led up to the moor.

The cold fog that always settled in the black hollows of the backstreets of St Bliz, wrapped her in a sooty swirl. Her dream was now fast dissolving in the dismal reality of the clammy early morning. Running warmed her up. She had a stray lump of sugar in her pocket, and two small bruised apples, carefully cut into quarters. She planned to go and search the rubbish boxes out the back of the village greengrocer on her way to school that morning.

Fred loomed out of the fog, standing by the fence looking up the valley and shifting uneasily from one hoof to another. Jenny skipped across the river, treading lightly on each of the round granite stepping stones and up the bank to the gate at the bottom of his field. He took the sugar from her outstretched hand with nervous, rubbery lips, his ears flicking back and forth. His muzzle looked as if it had been dipped in red pepper, the rest of his coat faded silver brown with a raggedy skimpy black mane and tail. In his day, he had been a grand little showjumper, but now he was very old and chewed up with cynicism.

Then Jenny heard it, a high ringing neigh. The sound came from further up the stream, on the edge of the moor that covered the backbone of the Cornish peninsula. She leapt back across the running water and hurried on up the path, listening through the thick mist that was gusting up the valley from the cold Atlantic. It took her five minutes to get to the wooden fence at the bottom field of Treloar farm.

4

There were no horses in the field, nor could she spot any in the smaller upper field that backed onto the high wall of the farm yard. But then she heard it again! A loud and unmistakable neigh that was coming from inside the yard. There must be a horse in one of the barns. She put her head on one side like a little bird, thinking, listening.

Everyone knew that Mrs Leigh who lived at Treloar farm had gone mad. They said she was no longer herself, suffering from dementia. Vanda Peregrine had come back to Cornwall and was there now, looking after her, and old Mrs Truelove from the dairy farm down the road helped as well. Perhaps it was Vanda's horse?

All Mrs Leigh's horses had been gone for some years now. But there was definitely a horse there this morning, perhaps it was one of the dream horses that were still tangled in Jenny's mind. She hopped around down on the path looking up at the farm house. The closed dark grey granite walls gave away no sign of what was happening within. After waiting for about twenty minutes she gave up and turned disconsolately, heading back home, to get ready for school. Halfway down the path she nearly jumped out of her skin when a huge grey shadow loomed up behind her.

"Hey, Jen, wanna lift?"

"Sure,'' she called back, grinning, recognising the horse and rider. It was Zane on his father's blue and white Gypsy cob stallion, Ghost. And he was exactly like a ghost this morning, blending in perfectly with the misty morning, his thick coat patched dark blue-grey and white in strange shapes.

Zane and Jenny were friends. He was eleven but taller and stronger than her as she was thirteen but small for her age. The two children were kindred spirits, they both loved horses. Zane only lived down in Cornwall a few months of the year with his father, Dane. The rest of the time he was banished back to inner city London with his neurotic, unreliable mother. As soon as he was old enough, he was planning to get a position as an apprentice jockey in a racing stable.

Jenny climbed onto the bank beside the path, ready to scramble up onto Ghost's reassuring broad back. Zane leant down and held out his

5

hand and helped to pull her on. The horse was as wide as he was tall, a huge 16 hh, with a chest like a barrel, and strong square legs, covered in hair called feathers. Jenny felt the warmth coming up through the thin denim jeans on her legs as she swayed behind Zane. She sniffed up the warm fetid odour of horse, her favourite smell in the whole world.

"There's a horse at old Missus Leigh's place," she told Zane.

"I know, that tall woman with the bright yella hair, she rode her up yesterday from across the moor aways. A big chestnut mare with four white legs, beautiful she is," said Zane, with the twang of the East Ender in his voice.

"That's amazing" exclaimed Jenny, her voice shrill and high with excitement.

"I was riding up by Hooting Carn. All she needed was a golden staff, or is it a ring thing that hangs from her waist?"

"I don't know," said Jenny. She knew of Vanda Peregrine, but she had never met her. She had only known Beatrice well enough to nod to in the street and call out "Good morning Mrs Leigh".

"I wish I'd known her before, you know when she had the horses," she said to Zane.

"Me Dad knew her a bit, she was going to get him to go up and plough those two fields on the hill."

"Did he do that, with Ghost here?" asked Jenny.

"No, she got ill, it didna' happen," replied Zane.

The rest of the ride passed in silence and Zane leaned back and pulled on the headcollar rope and the kind calm stallion stopped just near Jenny's back fence. He put his head down to nose around in the bitter grass that grew beside the path. He wouldn't eat this rubbish, he had grown fat on the rich valley grass up near the headland. Jenny slid off, landing neatly on her feet.

6

"Thanks heaps, see ya later," she called as she pushed her way back through the gap in the fence.

She stood on the back step and watched Ghost stride out down the path beside the stream, heading for home. Zane would be in no hurry. He didn't go to school when he stayed in Cornwall and he had all day to do as he chose. He would go back to his father's camp on the headland beyond St Bliz, above a small cove where the villagers swam in the summer. Jenny slipped inside and put some white sliced bread in the toaster for breakfast before her brothers and sisters got up. There was no jam or peanut butter, but she didn't care, she had a lot to think about. She spread the margarine on the hot toast and it melted in deliciously. She was cold after her morning out in the dank air. First, there had been her dream and now she had found out that there was a beautiful chestnut horse just arrived up at Treloar. Zane had said that it was a mare. She felt filled with irrational hope, she had dreamed it, and it was true, perhaps she was destined to ride the big chestnut mare.

Chapter Two

"Do ya 'av any stuff for the ponies?" asked Jenny at the green grocer, half an hour before she was due at St Bliz School.

"Sure, help yourself me luvver," said old Mr Mannering, a refugee from the Home Counties who self-consciously adopted the local idiom. He jerked his head towards the discarded fruit and vegetable crates at the back of the little square granite shop. Jenny smiled impishly at him. She had an enchanting pixie face with bright blue eyes, set slightly at an angle as if there was some oriental blood in her somewhere. She rushed around the back and rummaged through the crates with the leftovers and scraps and found enough old carrots and apples to fill two plastic bags. Perfect for Pablo, and certainly enough left for Fred, and perhaps she might get to see the new chestnut horse up at Treloar.

Wearing her crumpled, slightly grubby school dress and dirty old trainers she set off for school, hoping to waylay her new friend, the soppy girl Essie, who had arrived at St Bliz at the beginning of the year. Essie was a bit dim, but the good thing was that she owned a pony, a little black Dartmoor who was kept in her one-acre back garden on the western edge of the village, where the more expensive houses clustered as far away from the council estate as possible. Jenny soon discovered that Essie, who was a good six inches taller than her but skinny as a stick, was completely lacking in courage and determination. She was far too scared of Pablo to do anything at all with him. And in a way, this was perfectly understandable because Pablo was pure malevolence wrapped up in a small stout pony body, with teeth to bite, hoofs to kick and determined never ever to go the way that the rider wanted.

Jenny didn't care. She just wanted to be near a pony and Pablo was much better than nothing. She worked her magic friendliness on Essie who was inevitably a loner, not attractive, nor good fun and certainly not popular group material. Jenny's enthusiasm was so great that she had by dint of determination, rather than any sort of skill, got to the point where they could catch the pony, get the tack on and walk him

8

around the field. Essie had gone along with it all but had no faith in Jenny's unalterable belief that they would ultimately succeed in training the irascible pony. Pablo really was the most ferocious and unco-operative little animal.

Jenny had drawn up a training plan and every day she tried to achieve an objective. First, they had to catch him and this always took a while. They would corner him in the field - but it was tricky. He would let fly with both back feet, and the girls had the bruises to prove it. Once they had managed to slip on his rope halter by bribing him with apples and carrots they had a huge struggle to get the bridle on. It was an old, stiff leather thing with a rusty snaffle. Then they had to saddle him up with an equally old riding pad, with rusty stirrup irons and cracked girth straps. Essie would hold him while Jenny mounted. He would walk for a few steps, but if Jenny tried to turn him he would continue in a straight line with his head bent round, but not his body. He would halt at the gate and then the real struggle began. Jenny wanted to ride him up and down the road but he flatly refused to go out and would start to back up and even threatened to rear. It wasn't too scary because he was so small, not even 12 hh, so if Jenny slid down over his rump it wasn't far to the ground.

Essie was at the school gate, standing there forlornly, tall, and awkward looking. Her rather long nose was dripping and her pale brown hair hung lankly in the mist.

"Hi Essie!" called Jenny. "You won't believe it, there's a new horse up at Treloar farm!"

"What's it like?" asked Essie, without much enthusiasm.

"I don't know, but Zane said that it's chestnut, with white legs, I couldn't see it but I heard it."

Essie wasn't sure how to respond. Pablo had put her off horses and ponies for all time. She hadn't even really wanted a pony in the first place but her mother had produced him when they had first arrived, like a rabbit out of a hat, for their new rural life.

"Come on, let's go and find the others, I have to tell them!" said Jenny, dashing into the playground towards a large group of girls.

Essie trailed behind reluctantly. If it wasn't for Jenny there was no way she would have any chance to chat to the other girls. She really didn't like it much here at all. She wished they could go back to West Sussex, where her father still lived in their comfortable suburban house. She didn't understand at all why her mother had left him and dragged her down here.

The school day dragged on and finally the bell went. Jenny's excitement hadn't waned throughout the day and she dragged Essie back, so they could work on Pablo again. Unfortunately, Pablo was not in the mood, not in the mood at all. He didn't even want to be caught. He really didn't share the vision.

They chased him around the field, tempting him with bits of carrot and soft words but he was far too clever for them. He would snatch the titbit out of their hands and then turn his hindquarters towards them and they would leap aside before he double-barrelled them.

"He is the most annoying pony, I hate him!" said Essie petulantly after forty minutes. "Come on, let's go inside and go on the internet, I can't stand this another minute."

Jenny felt incredibly frustrated. Her dreams and reality just weren't matching up in any way.

"I've got to go home," she said reluctantly, thinking of the chocolate biscuits in Essie's larder and the solid-state laptop and fast internet connection. Her mother had made her promise to be back by five to look after the young children as she was off to a birthday celebration at the Angel Inn. There was to be a large crowd from the council estate, everyone was cousins with everyone else, and there were a great many Salmons spanning at least three, or even four generations.

Back home Jenny managed to marshal the younger kids and fed them baked beans on toast, with mugs of milky sweet tea. She found a packet of chocolate chip cookies at the back of the cupboard and settled them on the couch in front of the television with their favourite DVD.

She went back into the kitchen and was staring dispiritedly out the window, thinking about how hopeless their efforts with Pablo had been, when something flashed across her line of vision. It was the big chestnut mare, walking large as life down the path ridden by the woman with the long blond plait. It was like a sign, not to give up on her dreams.

She ran to the back door and watched as the impressive muscular haunches disappeared into the dusk. She was about to run after her but remembered she was in charge of her brothers and sisters. And what would she say anyway. But she took heart. She chose to believe that things would change, that the chance of a pony would come to her like a lucky talisman.

She stacked the plates into the dishwasher. She had this feeling that luck was coming her way. Eventually her mother came back from the pub.

"You know that Mrs Leigh, up at Treloar, she's only gone and kicked the bucket," she told Jenny, her voice a little slurred, her eyes glassy from drinking too much cider.

"Really, that is sad," said Jenny, but her mind was racing. Was that why the chestnut mare was up there? Who would live at Treloar now? Would they have more horses?

"So, the funeral is fixed for Saturday, and the whole village is goin', there's will be a big spread up at the Village Hall. Those women from the WI are organisin' the food."

"I suppose I'll go then," said Jenny, "I allus heard good things 'bout her, I wished that I had known her when she still had the horses. But what will I wear, you're meant to wear black to a funeral, aren't you?"

"We'll all go," said her mother. "As long as we're neat and tidy no-one is going to care what we wear. Never say no to a free feed and hopefully there'll be a bit more than cups of tea to drink."

That night Jenny lay in bed trying to slip back into her dream of the horses, she knew that if she wished and hoped enough it would come true. And she had seen the chestnut mare. She was sure it was a sign.

Chapter Three

Vanda Peregrine's inheritance should not have been a contentious issue, but somehow, she felt an utter fraud, not entitled to sole possession of Treloar farm and all Beatrice's belongings. But there was no-one contesting the will and she had just to get through the funeral and then decide what to do with the rest of her life.

The event had all been prearranged according to Beatrice's instructions, which were meticulously detailed as to hymns, no flowers and which guests were to be invited. In the front pew of the square granite church were the Dowager Duchess, old Mrs Bowles and Vanda reluctantly took her place beside them, feeling uncomfortable in a long black skirt and t-shirt that was too tight across her broad shoulders.

It was a windy hot summer day with thin white clouds scudding across the blazing sky. The mourners spilled out of the church and walked through the narrow streets to the clifftops. The distinctive sweet smell of the moors was edged with a salty tang from the sea. The sun beat down on Vanda's back, thick and warm like melted butter. She was the one to throw the ashes, flinging them out over the edge of the land. She felt awkward and nervous that the wind would dash them back into her face, very aware of the crowd watching her with self-conscious solemnity. The flurry of gritty, grey ash swirled out towards the sea and eddied down on the wind currents to the black-edged waves crashing below on the rocks.

Vanda was surprised that there were so many people. It seemed as if the whole village and many of the local farming folk had turned up. She whispered a good-bye to Beatrice feeling like a fraud, as if it were not her place. Then everybody was trooping back to the Village Hall for the wake. She walked a little apart from the others, then felt her arm being grasped rather too firmly, it was the Dowager Duchess. A whiff of lavender water, mixed with the unmistakeable sour odour of old lady.

"You know Beatrice and I have known each other since we were young gels," she said, in her commanding voice.

"Of course, I know she talked about you often and the hunting. You were both members of the hunt," Vanda said politely, feeling uncomfortable with the old lady's bony fingers hooking into the soft flesh of her arm. They marched along and then back on the tarmac, proceeding down the narrow winding street that led to the village hall.

"I'm sorry but I must go on and make sure that the catering is all arranged," Vanda said apologetically. Anything to get away from the old dragon. She slipped through the front door of the hall and saw to her relief that there were sandwiches, tea, coffee, cider, and cake for everyone. Vast plates were sat on white tablecloths on trestles, and every sort of sandwich, both white and brown bread, garnished with fresh parsley. It was a good spread and Beatrice would have been happy. Apparently, grief gave one an appetite thought Vanda who felt unutterably weary. She wondered when she might be able to slip away and get back to Treloar, when she was accosted by the other formidable old lady, Mrs Bowles.

"Why is it that you never wanted to join Goonhilly Pony Club? You know that Mrs Leigh would have been pleased to let you ride her horses to rallies and such like?" demanded the ancient old woman. Vanda felt her mouth open unattractively. Where had such a question come from? Perhaps death and funeral rites brought out the weirdness in everyone.

"I guess I'm just not a joining a club sort of person," she replied noncommittally, smoothing down her long flaxen plaits, which gave her the appearance of a Viking goddess. The last thing she felt she wanted to discuss was why she had never joined the pony club when she had been a teenager. Another wave of weariness swept over her. She just wanted to get out of there, grief for Beatrice was threatening to drown her. She had no desire for such a ridiculous conversation.

"But there are young people around here who could so much benefit from good instruction, in the same way as what Beatrice did for you," said Mrs Bowles warming to her favourite subject. She had come dressed in her customary mud-brown skirt with a drooping hemline,

14

a dirty-looking nylon shirt, and stout black lace-up shoes. Of course, she had an angle. It seemed everyone had an angle, thought Vanda.

"Last year Beatrice promised to hold a pony club camp at Treloar, just for the weekend."

"I see," said Vanda. Beatrice might very well have promised to hold a pony club camp. It was just the sort of jolly hockey sticks plan that would have appealed to her. But Vanda felt that any such promise was now rendered null and void.

"You have to honour her promise," said Mrs Bowles grimly. And Vanda saw that this was the dues, the price she had to pay for her inheritance.

"Well, what would it involve?" she asked, giving in if it meant that she could get out of here.

"No more than a dozen children, a weekend towards the end of August, during the school holidays. They camp in the field down by the stream and I'll organise the instructors. You could do the food."

"Is that a question or a statement?" asked Vanda dryly.

"What!" exclaimed Mrs Bowles.

"Yes, I can do the food," agreed Vanda resentfully. "Now that's arranged I must see to the other guests." She walked away, determined to get out of there before this irritating old woman tried to force her to agree to anything else. She didn't trust herself to keep her temper, or even worse breakdown in a storm of weeping that would look too grotesque, as if she was putting it on.

Thinking about it on the drive back up to the farm house, she had to concede that pony club was undoubtedly a 'good thing', promoting the care of horses and developing good horsemanship, which no doubt would have had the spill over effect of enabling children to develop moral characters. But it really was the least of her concerns right now. And the other side of the coin was that inevitably pony club members were encouraged to become competitive, to win and that might be considered not a 'good thing' at all. But such deep philosophical and moral matters were too much for her to ponder now. As a teenager, who had been taught to ride by Beatrice, she had eschewed the whole competitive thing. She loved horses, and of course wished that they were looked after properly, but she had never felt the need to prove to the world that she was a better rider than the next person. She simply loved riding for the way she could achieve some sort of natural harmony with a living animal and feel a part of nature on the moor and along the cliffs. The whole sitting up straight and getting the horse on the bit and jumping over a dozen obstacles had quite passed her by. She had always preferred to ride bareback with the horse just wearing a headcollar. She really wasn't interested in winning rosettes. Her joy in horses was a very private, almost spiritual thing.

Vanda vaguely remembered Goonhilly Pony Club when she was younger but then it had become almost defunct. She wondered if there really was a need for such an organisation in the area. Presumably most of the children were more into computer games, tip-tapping into their phones, shopping in Penzance or Truro. Consumerism seemed to be the dominant hobby of the masses these days.

She got back to Treloar and felt the peacefulness of the farm envelop her like soft comforting arms. The hot sun was gone but the evening was sweet-smelling and balmy. She walked down to the stream to see Clovelly. It would be easier to leave her out at night now that the weather was so warm, it would save the trouble of having to clean the stable. The mare was looking well, sleek, and shiny with a golden coat that seemed to capture the last rays of the sun. She had rounded out on the sweet green grass. Vanda did rather like her but there was something about her, a dark history. She had kicked her cousin Sofia's beloved brown thoroughbred gelding, Alfie, and he had had to be put down.

Now Sofia was back in Hampshire, and she had asked Vanda to look after the mare as she couldn't stand the sight of her. Something would have to be done - the animal couldn't stay here indefinitely. Vanda had decided she herself would leave soon. She would always come back but she had to go away. After the pony club camp in August.

16

Then it came to her, Sofia would be the one to help with this. Sofia was the ultimate pony club girl! Mrs Bowles had said she would organise the instruction but Vanda decided to make a bid for control, she would appoint Sofia to be the instructor, no matter what Mrs Bowles dictated. And then after the camp Sofia would have to take away Clovelly and that would solve that problem. Vanda found satisfaction in problem-solving when all the pieces came together in a logical order. She hated life to be messy. She had had enough of that with her scattered bipolar mother. That was what had been the worst with Beatrice, who had been there for her throughout her teenage years. That Beatrice should end up being fragmented, demented and not herself had been the worst of all ironies.

Then a shadow moved across the stream. In the half-light Vanda discerned a sprite-like form, a young girl. It was Jenny standing in the shadows, trying to get up the courage to step forward and talk to Vanda.

"Hello," called Vanda, letting the girl know that she had seen her.

"Hello," squeaked back Jenny, with a surge of excitement. She jumped up and down on the spot.

"I'm sorry about Mrs Leigh," she called out.

"Thank you," said Vanda, "I saw you at the funeral. What is your name?" The slight figure of the girl materialised in the darkening light in front of her.

"I'm Jenny Salmon, from St Bliz. That's a fair hansum chestnut mare."

"Yes, she is rather a magnificent creature, but not the easiest of characters. She killed my cousin's gelding Alfie, leastways she kicked and injured him and he had to be put down."

"That is very sad, but I'm sure she didn't mean it," said Jenny, always ready to believe the best of any horse.

"How can one tell the motivation of animal, it's a habit of anthropomorphising beasts of the field." Jenny was now totally

17

flummoxed, the way this woman talked it was like something off the BBC.

"I saw you ridin' her before," she said, desperate to get the conversation back to something that she could understand.

"Yes, I rode her down the stream out to the headland."

"That's where I live in the village, in one of the houses that backs onto the stream."

"I see," said Vanda.

Jenny hopped from one leg to another, but she couldn't see how to stretch this meeting further.

"I best be gettin' back for me tea," she said in the end.

"Bye then," said Vanda dismissively and turned to walk up the laneway to the farm house. She was aching with grief and melancholy. She filled a haynet with a mixture of lucerne and meadow hay, and carried it back down to tie to the gate for the mare. She checked the water in the trough and topped it up with a bucket from the stream. Slowly she trudged back up to the house. She would lock herself inside, shut herself away from the world, go up to bed and sleep. Her bones ached with weariness as if she were a hundred years old.

Upstairs she lay awake for a while, motionless, breathing lightly watching the moonlight glance through the gingham check curtains. It was still light outside, a strange washed-out illumination. A perfect night for lovers. She wondered whether Dane was sitting around his campfire. She had only been up to see him once, and he had been reserved, even taciturn. She tried to reason with herself. This was just his way. She sighed, and turned her mind back to her own future. She would stay in Cornwall until probate was through and spend her time going through Beatrice's things. Then she would be free to travel. She would go back to writing the script of her own life.

She had decided that she would never sell Treloar, well not in the foreseeable future. It was a backstop, a bolt hole, associated with the best of her rather mixed childhood memories. She had never had this type of security before. Thinking of material security her mind drifted to Sofia. She had only met her cousin for the first time a few months ago. Their mothers had been sisters and Sofia had been brought up in Hampshire with her father and her step-mother. In fact, she quite liked her cousin, who was, to say the least, not at all bookish – rather pragmatic, materialistic driven solely by the desire to win horse competitions. To Vanda this was a strange, but rather fascinating mindset.

Chapter Four

Essie's mother, Belinda Lampton, enjoyed her job working in the council offices over the moor at Penzance. The Thursday after the funeral she was sitting in the little staffroom, self-consciously reading The Cornishman newspaper, trying to fit in with the locals. An advertisement caught her eye. It asked for children interested in attending Goonhilly Pony Club camp to contact Mrs Bowles on a St Ives number.

"This would be just perfect for Essie," said Belinda to the disparate group of her colleagues who were drifting in and out, making themselves cups of tea and coffee.

"What dear?" asked comfortable old Mrs Grimsby who had worked there for at least the last hundred years.

"Pony club, it's just thing for our Essie, she's got no confidence, she hasn't quite got to grips with her pony Pablo. Apparently, he's rather stubborn."

"Well pony club sounds just the thing, I remember years ago, the Goonhilly Pony Club was one of the best in Cornwall, used to win the regional gymkhana awards sweeping the board."

"Well, it would be nice for Essie to socialise with other children, at the moment she just has Jenny, who is very sweet but she's off the council estate." There was a social divide between the council estate tenants and those who lived in the private houses in the village. Belinda had forgotten that a number of her colleagues lived in council estate housing.

"Who is running it now, is it still old Mrs Bowles?"

"Yes, that's what it says here, I'm going to ring her," said Belinda, pressing the numbers on her mobile phone.

*****

So, when Essie's mother got back from work that evening, she told Essie that she was to join Goonhilly Pony Club and attend the weekend summer camp. It was being held up at Treloar farm on the third weekend of August, the one before the Bank Holiday weekend.

"That sounds good," Essie responded tentatively. "But I hope that Pablo will behave himself."

"But of course, he will darling, they will help you to train him, and it's meant to be the best fun, and there are three brothers, the Tregonning family from a big dairy farm over at Sennen coming. The youngest, Tom is twelve, just one year younger than you, then the middle one Dominic, apparently he's artistic, and the eldest Nick, he is almost a man now, working full-time on his father's farm."

Her mother ran on but Essie was a bit slow on the uptake. She processed this information slowly but didn't feel hugely encouraged. She was always nervous around boys and had no idea what to say to them.

"Do you think Jenny could come too?" she asked, hoping for some moral support.

"Well she doesn't have a pony," said her mother, thinking that the best part of this plan was that Essie would meet some other children, not be quite so involved with Jenny.

"Well I'm sure I've heard of unmounted members, can you give me the number and I'll pass it on to her," said Essie.

"Oh, all right, here it's in my phone," said her mother resignedly. Perhaps, it was rather unkind of her to want Jenny to miss out. Belinda didn't understand that in fact, it had been Jenny's universal popularity that had eased Essie into a new group of friends. Jenny made it her business to be liked by everyone.

*****

The next day at school Essie rushed over to Jenny and told her about the camp and handed over a scrap of paper.

"Perhaps you could go as an unmounted member," she suggested.

"That sounds brilliant, but how much does it cost?" asked Jenny, her heart beating faster. It was as if every time there was an opportunity to do something with horses she just missed out.

"Oh, I didn't ask," said Essie, thinking how hopeless she was. She knew that Jenny didn't have much money. "Well - you can just ring up and find out. You know it's going to be up at Treloar farm, that's not far from the village is it. Apparently, that woman that's inherited the farm, is letting Goonhilly Pony Club go there for the camp."

"Yes, I know Treloar," said Jenny, perhaps this was finally her chance to get to know Vanda better. Essie went on and described the Tregonning boys from the dairy farm.

"Yes, of course, I know of them," said Jenny, who knew everyone, especially anyone with a horse, within a fifty-mile radius of St Bliz. The morning bell rang and they hurried into class. Jenny resolved she would borrow her cousin's mobile at break time and ring the number, she absolutely had to go. She had just about £100 saved up, which she was hoping to put towards the purchase of a pony, but it would be worth it, to spend it on this camp.

*****

That weekend Jenny and Essie sat down and tried to work out how they might transform Pablo into a well-behaved pony. They looked up napping on the internet and there were warnings about a horse spinning and rearing. There was a list of possible reasons such as ill-fitting tack, discomfort, fear, but none of these seemed to apply and lastly there was disobedience, which seemed about right for the stubborn little pony.

"The best solution seems to be to ride out with another horse and Pablo will follow, like the herd instinct," said Jenny.

"But how do we find another horse and rider?" asked Essie plaintively.

"Well perhaps Zane could bring Ghost down, he seems pretty steady."

"Well you could ask him, but I'm not sure that Mummy likes Zane and his father, she says that they're Gypsies."

"Well I'll ask him, but there's no-one else, although there is that woman Vanda up at Treloar, she's been ridin' that chestnut mare aroun' a bit, I s'ppose I could go up and ask her."

"Vanda would be better than that Zane," concluded Essie.

"We could get behind 'im with a long whip, or if I ride 'im, you come up behind and wave the stick," said Jenny doubtfully. It sounded a bit drastic, but they had to do something.

"I'm not sure that I could do that," said Essie doubtfully. "Anyway, what we need is a lunge whip and we don't have one, I suppose I could ask Mum to buy me one."

"Well you ride 'im and I'll use a long stick, we'll cut one down from a tree."

"That sounds even worse, what if he starts rearing? That is meant to be one of the worst vices," said Essie. The real problem was that she was scared and Pablo knew it. He was getting the better of them every time and it made her feel so helpless, and she didn't have much confidence in Jenny either.

*****

The next day at school there was the usual end of term activities. The long summer holidays loomed ahead. Jenny's brain was buzzing with speculation about the camp. Perhaps there would be a spare pony that she would be able to ride. Then there was the problem that she had to actually learn to ride. She'd been up on Ghost behind Zane, and she had walked Pablo around but had never trotted or cantered. She resolved to go up to see Zane about getting him and Ghost to help them make Pablo go. She felt too shy at the thought of approaching Vanda.

Finally, the going home bell went and she was walking out the school gate. She looked across the road and there was Zane. That was weird, Zane usually avoided coming anywhere near the children in the village, and certainly not hanging around the school. She hurried over to talk to him.

"There's that dirty Pikey boy that's living up in that van with his father, would you believe it?" said one of the girls in her class, her voice bitchy and disdainful.

"Jen!" he called as she approached. Other children turned around to look and she slid up beside him. They hurried off down towards the square, to get away from the others.

"Me Dad has got three new horses, and there's one for you to ride!" The words came out in a rush. Jenny stood stock still and stared at him. All thought of the public embarrassment of being seen with him disappeared in a flash.

"What did yer say?"

"There's one for you to ride, he's ever so nice, quiet, a pink colour."

"A pink colour," repeated Jenny, visualising an improbable pretty Mr Little Pony with a long silver mane and tail.

"Yes, a red roan, and I gotta a blue roan and Dad has got this little stallion, who is causin' a lot of trouble. We're gonna ride them and train 'em up and sell 'em, and you can ride the little strawberry one. He's ever so quiet, I rode 'im yesterday."

Jenny clutched her hands together as if thanking God. Finally, this was her chance! It was like a pony had just dropped down from heaven right into her lap.

It took them about ten minutes to get back to the camp where Zane lived with his father, through the village and along the rough track that led to the headland. The colourful Gypsy caravan looked like something out of a picture book. Painted yellow hoops over a green canopy with red ornamental designs.

Jenny wished she'd had a chance to dash home for her jeans, she was wearing a school dress, she would just have to ride in that. It didn't matter, her own pony to train, or rather to learn to ride. This was her big chance! Perhaps, if he weren't sold by the end of summer, she could take him to the pony club camp. A vista of possibilities streamed through her mind.

They ran along the track that sloped down the side of the valley to the flat area of land where there was a campfire built of stones with a metal tripod, from which hung an old blackened kettle. Placed on a large flat rock was a huge saucepan, like a cauldron, in which Dane would cook rabbit stews, or beef that he bought from the St Bliz butcher. The horses were tied in a line strung between two stubby gorse bushes. At the other end of the camping area, Ghost was tethered in the long grass, swishing his thick tail to drive away the annoying insects. Jenny could see that there were two smaller ponies, one pink and one blue and a bigger bright brown horse with a jet-black mane and tail. She assumed that the smallest one on the end, which did indeed look pink, was the pony she was to ride. He wasn't at all tall, but bigger than Pablo, perhaps 13 hh.

Chapter Five

Zane's father was very weather-beaten, tall and angular, and with his battered hat he could have been a wizard out of Harry Potter. He was putting a saddle on the back of the bigger bay pony. According to Zane, this indomitable, tough, little creature was a stallion and proving to be something of a challenge.

"Hi Dad! You gonna ride 'im then," said Zane, dumping his rucksack down by the side of the caravan.

Jenny approached slowly. She never knew how to talk to Dane, she felt intimidated by him. He was so silent and stern. He was concentrating on fitting the saddle. Taking the saddle cloth and pulling it up into the gullet so that it didn't press down on the withers, then stretching out each of the horse's front legs so that the loose skin behind the elbows didn't feel uncomfortable with the tightened girth.

Jenny felt as if she was moving through a dream, hardly daring to believe that she really was going to get to ride. It was as if she could touch the shining burning joy in the air around her. The little pink pony was peeping out from behind a large gorse bush. She walked over to him and saw that he had sweet, little, pricked ears and the most enormous kind dark eyes that were watching her trustingly. She patted him and he accepted her caresses. He really was a most unusual colour, when she looked carefully she could see that his coat was a mixture of brown, black, white, and chestnut hairs which is what made him look pink. His legs, face and thick tail were all black. If she had been more knowledgeable she would have noticed that his head was a little coarse, his back a little long, and his tail sprouted from his rump awkwardly, not in a single flowing line. But that wouldn't have mattered at all, he was a pony, living, breathing, sweet-natured, and for her to ride.

"He looks absolutely fab!" she burst out in a shrill voice. But Zane and Dane were concentrating on the bright bay stallion who was snorting and standing with his legs braced. He looked like an unexploded bomb about to orbit into space. Zane held him as his

26

father mounted. He was up on his back in one fluid movement and the gelding stood stock still, then he threw himself into the air in a series of stiff-legged bucks with all four feet off the ground, his head pushed down between his front legs. Jenny stood there watching, she had never seen anything like it. Dane sat as if glued to the saddle, his long legs wrapped around the horse, and eventually he managed to wrench its head up and they set off at a jolting canter around the floor of the valley. They passed Ghost who kept his head down grazing, he had seen it all before. After about ten minutes the chunky little bay stallion seemed to run out of steam, his spirit quenched, a least temporarily, and he walked back towards them sweating. Dane sat him quietly.

"Don't worry about Berry 'ere," said Zane to Jenny patting the little pink gelding. "He's good to ride, quiet in traffic, bomb-proof. We'll saddle up and take 'em up on the moor. This blue one, she's a beauty, they said she was in foal to the stallion. We've called him Himself because he's so full of 'imself. He's going to be castrated soon. Only Dad will ride him at first."

Jenny turned this information over in her mind. She was thinking that the pink horse would probably get sold quickly, he was so quiet and so pretty, he would fetch good money. If only she could keep riding him until the camp. If only she could buy him, but she had hardly any money at all and still had to pay for the pony club membership. She took hold of the lead rope and ran her hand down the front of Berry's face. He was watching her curiously, with no trace of fear. Unlike the blue mare, who looked distinctly uneasy, shifting her weight from one hoof to another, her ears swivelling nervously. She was very pretty, much prettier and more elegant than Berry, with a dished face, thick black eyelashes framing large liquid dark eyes and a dainty little muzzle. Jenny wondered what the foal would look like with two such good-looking parents, it would be fantastic if it came out blue as well, rather than the more common bay colour, although that bay horse was a lovely bright nut-brown.

"Will I put the saddle on?" she asked doubtfully.

"Yes, use that little straight knee brown saddle over there," said Zane jerking his head to the pile of tack. It was a child's leather show saddle, quite flat with hardly any knee pads, made of fine-grained pigskin leather. Nothing like the ugly riding pad that they used for Pablo.

"An' the bridle?"

"Yes, there as well, just a snaffle bridle with single reins, nothin' compl'cated."

"Awright," said Jenny quietly, wondering if she would be able to work out how it all went together. Fortunately, Berry stood there quietly and co=operatively. He even dropped his head when she held the bridle up. It felt like he was wishing her well. After she had managed to get the bridle on she placed a woollen saddle blanket on his back and then carefully positioned the saddle on top. She reached tentatively down under his round barrel tummy and got hold of the girth and just managed to do up the buckles. She was paranoid about twisted girths and went around the other side to make sure that it was lying flat. She tried to tighten it up but thought perhaps he was holding his breath.

"Don't worry, when ya get on 'e let his breath out, then we'll pull the girth up a few more 'oles," said Zane.

Before she mounted, she adjusted the stirrup leathers, Zane had ridden him yesterday and they were far too long. She shortened them up three holes and tried this out for size by putting the tips of her fingers on the metal bar where they were attached to the saddle and stretched them down to her armpit, perhaps just one hole shorter. She went around to the other side and shortened that one up as well. Then she stood in front of him and checked that they were both the same length. She had read somewhere that with old tack sometimes the left-hand stirrup leather would stretch and be longer. They both seemed the same.

"C'm on, mount up!" said Zane holding the rein for her. She scrambled on and then Zane pushed her leg forward so he could get under the saddle flap to tighten the girth.

28

"Another three 'oles," he said. Then he swung up onto the blue mare with the same lithe and effortless movement as his father. Blue was shifting around suspiciously, not standing still and obediently, as Berry was doing.

Jenny took a rein in each hand, making sure to hold them correctly, then she closed her legs against Berry's round sides, just a tentative signal to go forward. He didn't move. She tried again using a little more vigour. He stepped forward. She arranged herself in what she thought was a correct position, she needed to push her heels down, her back straight, looking between his ears.

"Relax," said Zane, smiling at her. "I's not a ridin' class, it's meant to be fun."

"What is that one like?" asked Jenny. "What is 'er name?"

"It's Blue. She's a bit of an 'andful. I'll be relyin' on you and Berry to give her a lead, show 'er 'ow to behave."

"Is your father bringing that stallion out with us?" asked Jenny a little doubtfully, it didn't look like that fiery creature would be a good example for any other horse.

"Yep, we'll all goin' together, up along the top of the cliffs."

"Fab," said Jenny. They walked side by side along the track that went across the floor of the valley, then turned l eft onto the path that led around the cliffs. Jenny twisted around in the saddle and saw that Dane and the brown stallion were following at a distance.

"Let's trot," said Zane. Jenny didn't say anything. She didn't want to admit that she'd never trotted before. She just had to find the rhythm, going up and down in time with the two-beat movement. She'd studied how to do it a lot with her hardback picture book that explained how to ride. She put both reins in one hand, screwed her face up in concentration and held firmly onto the pommel of the saddle, just in case.

"You go first, we'll follow," she said to Zane. She didn't want him to watch her. Berry trundled along behind Blue, Jenny bumped and bounced, trying desperately to get the rhythm. Then she found it for two strides and missed it again and started bumping. Berry didn't seem to notice. Perhaps he had already taught lots of children to ride.

"You ready to canter?" shouted Dane over his shoulder, and then Blue sprang away, bounding, twisting and turning along the path.

"Gosh!" gasped Jenny, but Berry broke into what felt like the most wonderful, smooth, rocking-horse canter. Jenny gave up trying to steer with the reins and held on to the pommel with both hands, pulling upwards so she was drawn down into the deepest part of the seat of the saddle, rocking with the rhythmical feeling. It felt wonderful! The wind was rushing and whizzing across her face and she could hear Berry's small black hoofs thudding on the hard ground. This was a miracle! It was better than she had ever dreamed, she was cantering! She felt exultant.

When they got to the top of the hill Zane managed to pull Blue back to a walk and Berry obediently slowed behind her. Then, Jenny nearly did fall off, but just managed to cling on.

"That was the most fantastic feeling," she gasped, using one hand to grab a thick strand of mane to rebalance herself. Zane turned around and grinned at her.

"Do ya want to swap ponies?" he asked, teasing her.

"Not in a million years, this is the most adorable sweet lovable pony in the whole world." She reached down and patted Berry's neck. She felt her heart about to burst with love and pride that she had finally trotted and cantered and hadn't fallen off.

Zane didn't suggest that they went any faster than a walk for the rest of the ride. Dane was no longer behind them, presumably he'd gone off on his own. Jenny and Zane circled around gorse bushes, every now and then coming out at the edge of the cliffs with a panoramic view of the sea that was flat and grey, the horizon smudged and fading into the sky. Blue's behaviour didn't improve, she just wouldn't settle, but Zane was endlessly patient. Berry plodded on reassuringly and Jenny sat in the saddle in a daze of happiness.

"Ya stoopid, stoopid girl, you know you're not really scared a' all," Zane said soothingly to Blue as she propped, trying to swing around.

"I really don't know how you manage to stay on sometimes," said Jenny wonderingly. She hadn't realised before quite what a wonderful rider Zane was. It was almost dark when they got back to the camp.

"Mum's gonna be wonderin' what's 'appened to me," she said.

"Then go now, don't worry I'll sort out the ponies, Dad'll 'elp me. But you'll come down tomorrow straight after school?" he asked.

"Yes of course," said Jenny, a huge smile spread across her face. It was a fair distance back to the village but she managed to run most of the way. No-one at home had even noticed that she was late and she slipped in to help her mother dish up the dinners and set them down the long table bench on one side of the living room. The other four children were sitting in a bunch on the couch watching Corrie.

"Come on you kids, come and get your dinner!" called their mother. Jenny sat in the corner of the couch and ate her sausages, mash, and baked beans without tasting a mouthful. She had so much to think about, she couldn't believe what had happened today. She'd trotted and cantered and it had all been miraculous. Finally, her dreams were coming true. She hugged her secret to herself, the others just wouldn't understand, it was too special to be shared. After dinner, she collected up the plates and carried them out to the dishwasher. She helped her mother load it and then started on the frying pan in the sink.

"Thanks Jenny," said her mother, looking at her for a moment. "Are you all right?"

"Do you mind if I run over to Essie's I've got to talk to her about something?" she asked, avoiding the question.

"Whatever," said her mother distracted by two of the boys scuffling and fighting over the remote in the doorway. "Hey, you two, cut it out!" she called.

Jenny slipped out the front door and ran down the street into the centre of the village and then cut across to Essie's house. She was just bursting with the news. Essie was sitting disconsolately on the sofa, watching television.

"Hi Essie!" said Jenny.

"You didn't come today, you went off with Zane," said Essie pouting a little. Jenny smiled her sweet forgive-me smile.

"You'll never guess, there's three ponies up at Zane's place, his Dad bought them at the Camborne horse sale.

"Wow! Three? Do you think you could ride up so that they give Pablo a lead, you know, what we had planned?" she asked plaintively. Jenny felt stricken, in all the excitement she had quite forgotten about the problem with Pablo.

"Sure," she replied. "Of course, I'll ask Zane tomorrow. We can ride all summer over the moor, and down to the coves to swim."

"Do you really think Pablo will co=operate?" asked Essie doubtfully.

"I think he might, if we handle him the right way. And Zane can help. He can ride anything."

They sat next to each other, the television droned on in front of them.

"Oh, hello Jenny," said Essie's mother coming in, "I thought I heard your voice, you know Essie has to get ready for bed."

"Of course, sorry to stay so late, see ya," said Jenny smiling sweetly. "Anyways, me Mum will be wondering where I've got to. I'll see you at school tomorrow then Essie."

She left quickly and ran off down the street, over to the other side of the village. She slipped inside and drifted up the stairs and sat on her bed her school books spread out around her. She just wanted to relive every minute of her ride this afternoon. Tomorrow she would take her jeans and t-shirt in her bag.

Chapter Six

Jenny woke with the name 'Berry' on her lips, the word materialised in her mind, as white as angels' wings. She felt guilty but she didn't bother to go up and see Fred. He wouldn't really miss her. Lying in bed she thought about riding this afternoon. By rights she should ask Zane if they could go and help Essie, but most of all she wanted to practise trotting and cantering. There was so much to learn and messing around with feeble Essie and Pablo would be wasting time.

School dragged so slowly that day. She sat chewing her pen daydreaming, and several times the teacher asked a question and it all completely passed her by. Finally, the going home bell rang and she rushed outside. She headed off through the village and towards the headland. From the top of the valley she could see the ponies in the distance standing together next to the gorse bushes, all saddled up and ready to go.

"You're so lucky not going to school," she said puffing a little when she got to the camp. Zane sat on a little wooden stool beside the bright fire, stirring a stew in the big cauldron while she disappeared behind a bush to get changed. Then they went over to the ponies to untie the reins calling to Dane that they were off. The tall silent man stalked away, wearing a brown, wrinkled, long, waxed-cotton jacket, that matched his face as if they had both been through a hundred Cornish winter storms.

"You know it actually ge's a bit lonely down here, just with me Dad, we don't 'ave a telly or anythin'," said Zane to Jenny, out of earshot of his father.

"Oh, I suppose so, you know you're welcome to come over to our house, there's loads of people comin' and goin'," said Jenny, wondering what it must be like to feel lonely. Sometimes she would have given anything to have some privacy.

The two of them rode north this time, towards Sennen, along the top of the cliffs. Berry behaved impeccably, walking quietly, not looking to right nor left, unlike Blue, who danced and cavorted and several times looked like she was about to throw herself over the cliff edge and down onto the slick black rocks below, where the water angrily crashed and foamed. Seagulls screeched above them and the wind rushing in from the sea was very cold. Finally, the path meandered inland a little and flattened out.

"Come on let's trot, you've got to practise you know - rising trot, up, down, up down," said Zane trying to help her. This time, she managed to get into the rhythm and mainly kept to it, just bumping a little.

"You know you're gonna to be a really good rider one day Jen," said Zane encouragingly.

"Thank you for saying that but I just have to practise more."

"Well, you can ride every day for a while anyways, until we sell Berry that is. Dad's talkin' about keeping Blue until she has the foal, so I'll just ride her for now and then after she's 'ad it he's gonna decide what to do. 'E might even keep her and she could 'ave another one with Ghost, breed somethin' a bit bigger, be worf more, a bigger foal."

"That would be fab!" said Jenny, wishing that Berry was a mare and there was a chance of keeping him. They trotted again several times and she felt herself improving. Then they cantered. This time, she held on to the pommel with only one hand, the other holding the reins. It was that same miraculous smooth, rocking feeling. Perhaps Zane was right and one day she would be a good rider. Ahead of her Blue didn't seem to be settling down at all. She snorted and pranced like a giddy goat and let fly with her back feet, bucking, just narrowly missing Berry's head. Berry took absolutely no notice. He seemed immune to her silliness. The path widened so they could ride two abreast.

"You know next week Dad said that we'll get the vet in to castrate the little bay stallion. That should help him to settle down a bit. I'm going to help when they do the operation."

"Wow. That sounds massive. I'm not sure that I could do that."

"I've gotta go back to London at the en' of the summer," said Zane, his voiced edged with wistfulness. "You know it's another world up there."

"I've never even bin to London," said Jenny.

"It's full of cars and fumes and shops and people and huge towering grey blocks of flats and everywhere people all colours of the rainbow, and 'ardly any grass, 'cept in the parks. The thing I miss the most is the 'orses and me Dad of course. Even though it does get a bit borin' here, at least I've got the 'orses."

"I guess you would," said Jenny not quite sure what to say. She couldn't imagine a life away from her noisy argumentative family. She didn't want to ask Zane about his mother. She always got the feeling that she wasn't all that motherly. It made her feel awkward.

"You know if you lived down here you could go to school in the village," she said hopefully.

"No, the deal is that I can only come in the holidays. Mum needs me," said Zane. He sounded almost grown up then as if his mother were the child. Jenny didn't understand it at all.

"I saw Essie last night," she said. "Do you think we could ride over and then she could come with us on Pablo. I've been tryin' to help her with 'im but he's a little monster, perhaps you could make him go."

"I s'ppose so," said Zane, not sounding very enthusiastic. "Maybe durin' the 'olidays," he agreed half-heartedly. "Let's go!" he called to change the subject.

He dug his heels into Blue's sides, leaning forward like a whippet-thin jockey crossing the finishing line at Cheltenham. Berry took off behind them and Jenny had never galloped so fast. She copied Zane, leaning forward with a firm grasp of Berry's thick black mane, half-standing in the stirrups. Her eyes were blurred with tears from the wind and she could see Blue's flashing rump up ahead of her. She wasn't steering, rather staying on while Berry swerved this way and that along the narrow twisting path.

Eventually, they got back to the camp and Jenny found herself breathless with exertion. She'd never really thought about how physically demanding riding was. Determined to do her bit, she stayed to help with the unsaddling. They went down to the stream and filled buckets with fresh water, staggering back to the camp where Dane not having any mesh cooling rugs, covered the loins of each of the ponies with a thick hessian sack.

"Lead them round til they cool down," he said brusquely with more than a hint of criticism. Both ponies were hot and steaming, not clipped, and not yet that fit. After about twenty minutes Zane was satisfied. Jenny carried the buckets of feed to each of the four horses and they all looked pleased to see her, even level-headed Ghost looked at her with an enthusiastic expression on his broad face. Blue and Berry nudged at her and whinnied and nickered deep in their throats. Dane had mixed up their feeds, mainly chaff with a couple of cups of crushed barley, a splash of diluted molasses, a dash of corn oil and a handful of coarse salt. Zane had told her that Dane had bought some chaff and barley from an old farmer near Zennor, using his caravan to go and collect it and cart it back. Apparently, he disapproved of pre-mixed feeds. He liked to know exactly what they were getting.

"We'll tether them down the valley tonight," said Dane curtly. "There's some good fresh grass there. You do that Zane when they finish their feeds, you better get on home," he nodded at Jenny. The sun had sunk below the horizon, early summer dark was coming on, pink and apricot streaks spread out across the sky promising good weather tomorrow. Reluctantly Jenny took her leave, the stew smelled tasty, but it was obvious that she was not invited. Leastways, she had to get home to her own dinner. It took longer than she thought hurrying through the half-light, the muscles in her legs seemed to have stretched unnaturally.

But no-one noticed or said anything when she got home. She found her plate of dinner in the oven, corn beef hash with soggy cabbage, soaked with lumpy white sauce. But she didn't care, all she could think about was Berry and the amazing feeling she had experienced on that final gallop back to the camp. She felt as if her blood was running fast and red around her body. She had always known that riding horses was the meaning of life. It was magical, that was the best way to explain it. She imagined herself as some sort of mythical princess crossed with a centaur, at one with her steed. With Berry, it was so easy, he must be the kindest pony in the world. She couldn't quite imagine being able to handle Blue who seemed to be jerked around with invisible electrical wires like a wild-eyed puppet. She went to bed early, before it was dark and resolutely shut her mind to the thought of when Berry would be sold.

Chapter Seven

Vanda watched as Clovelly Princess roamed around the bottom field restlessly swishing her tail at imaginary flies and flattening her ears and throwing her head around as if she was grazing in a herd of imaginary horses. The mare had been staying at Treloar for several weeks now and although Vanda was riding her every day she hadn't settled. She wasn't the settling down type and, as unfriendly as she was to other horses, she didn't like being alone.

Vanda had been riding her bareback down the stream path, jogging past the council houses and on into the valley where Dane was camped. If he came out of the caravan then she would greet him and they would talk, at least for a minute or two. But more often he didn't make an appearance and she knew that he was there and choosing not to speak to her. She told herself that he was taciturn, unconventional and she only admired him for his principles. She approved of the way that he eschewed the luxuries of modern life. But the truth was that she dreamed that one day they might get together. But she hardly acknowledged these thoughts even to herself, and she made sure never to betray them to him. More than anything she dreaded rejection. She would wait forever rather than make the first move and declare herself.

The hazy summer days lengthened and drifted by. It was pleasant enough, certainly in contrast to the tension of the spring, when she had been waiting for Beatrice to die. But it didn't feel real. She was aware of her own evasion of the sharp edges of life. She was failing to grasp the nettle. She had to plan, to do something. A career would have been the conventional choice after graduating with a first-class honours degree. She could go on to post-grad, perhaps a Phd, become a doctor. Doctor Vanda Peregrine. It just didn't sound right. In fact, it sounded ridiculous.

In the meantime, the only duty she had, besides caring for the big chestnut mare, was to arrange the pony club camp and after that she hoped her future would reveal itself to her. She was dreading the camp, it was just so not her. She decided to ring her cousin and picked up her mobile.

"Sofia, how are you?"

"Oh Vanda, I was just thinking about you. I'm fine thank you."

Of course, Sofia was lying, there was an awkward pause.

"Clovelly is here you know, she's been here for a while now."

"Yes, how is she?" asked Sofia, unable to keep the hate and spite out of her voice.

"She's fine. I've been riding her a bit around the moor but I think you need to think about her future, you see I'm going away in a couple of months."

"Yes, of course, I'll work something out and let you know." Sofia was about to hang up.

"Well actually," said Vanda annoyed at Sofia's childish attitude. "I was hoping that you might be able to come down and stay for a while, you see there's this pony club camp to be held here the third weekend in August and I was rather hoping that you might help. You see there's this old dragon, Mrs Bowles, she is running it and I really can't face her on my own."

"Do you mean coming to visit you at Treloar, where you're looking after that old woman?" Sofia asked, instinctively screwing up her nose in distaste.

"Well no, I didn't mention it but Beatrice has died, but yes I did mean Treloar, I'm living here." She paused for a moment. "By myself, well with Clovelly."

In the normal course of events Sofia would have been in no hurry to get back down to Cornwall. But on the other hand, staying with Vanda at Treloar during the summer might be quite pleasant. And things here in Hampshire had not turned out as she had hoped. The superstar three-day eventing horse, Gullivers Travels, on which she was meant to be competing, was now out of action, without her

39

getting him to a single event. He'd strained a ligament. In fact, she would be glad of an excuse to get away for a while. Against all expectations, her life now was rather mundane. Officially she was working for her step-mother, Henrietta at Estrella Stables. But with no horse to compete on she was doing routine stable work and breaking in young horses with Sarah, the head girl. It had turned out that it was not much fun. Of course, she would have to clear it with Henrietta but she could make the excuse that Vanda needed her help.

"I'd have to check with Henrietta, but perhaps she would let me come down for a while," she replied. "Can I ring you back later, I'll see what I can arrange."

Sofia put her phone back in her pocket and thought about it. She could see some charm in the idea. She was bored, working full days at the stables for a paltry wage as an assistant head girl, which as far as she was concerned was nothing more than a lowly groom. And being polite to Henrietta was a drag. The transition from privileged daughter of the house to full-time employee at the stables had not been much fun, if not exactly humiliating, it was definitely a comedown.

At first when she had been training Gully with the expectation of winning international level three-day events she had been overjoyed, dreaming of gold medals. Now Gully was probably out of action for the rest of this year and it had all become rather dull. And there was the question of that wretched Clovelly Princess. She was going to have to decide. She could always get the mare sent back here to Hampshire. She could even try competing with her but she hated the thought of her. She still hadn't forgiven the evil bitch for killing her beloved brown gelding Alfie. But then, if she sold her, she could perhaps buy herself another horse. She decided to broach the subject of spending some time down at Cornwall with Henrietta at dinner that night.

"I've had a call from Vanda Peregrine down in Cornwall," she said introducing the topic over an extremely healthy, if rather unappetising, chicken salad that evening. She kept her eyes down, feeling her step-mother's gaze fixing upon her.

"Yes, Vanda, she is your cousin, I remember you mentioned her," said Henrietta, as always impeccably polite, if not particularly approachable or warm.

"Yes, that's right, her mother was my mother's sister. Anyway, she's been looking after that chestnut mare and I've got to do something about her. And Vanda's got herself roped into hosting a pony club camp and has asked if I could go down and help."

Sofia took another mouthful of salad, rather limp sad lettuce and cut up tomatoes that were peculiarly tasteless, with a mere drizzle of low-fat salad dressing. She assumed her most neutral expression. She knew that Henrietta would undoubtedly approve of her helping in a voluntary activity. Henrietta was always one for good works in the village.

"Well, I don't see why not. You could take Nat down, that three-year old, he's the most advanced in his education. You could ride him on the moors, take him over to Max Winters' cross-country course, a change of scene would certainly bring him on. Helping with a pony club camp sounds good, you could gain some experience doing a bit of instructing, and of course there's the family thing. Vanda sounds like an interesting person."

Sofia smiled a little at that. 'An interesting person' was an expression that covered a whole host of possibilities. The fact that she had told Henrietta that Vanda had gone to university and was something of an intellectual no doubt appealed to Henrietta, who had to be the world's biggest snob. Henrietta might even suppose that Vanda could be a good influence. Sofia had bombed her A levels a year ago, and Henrietta knew that she was going to have to do something about it, but when it came to Sofia she felt depressed and helpless. No amount of reproving suggestions seemed to achieve anything. On the other hand, her own daughter, Allegra was set to go to the London School of Economics in the autumn. Allegra had always been a perfectly behaved child. The opposite of Sofia. Whereas Sofia was tall with endless long legs and a very smooth olive complexion, long curly black hair, and amazing green eyes: Allegra was short and curvy, almost plump, blonde, blue-eyed, sweet, well-behaved and very good at schoolwork. Now to top it all Allegra was being courted by Tristan Littleton, the heir to Penmar Hall. Strangely, the old-fashioned notion of courtship was an apt description of Tristan who seemed to be living his life according to the social values of pre-war Britain.

"Also, of course, you know that Allegra is staying down at Penmar Hall with Tristan's family this summer, I think it would be good if you got to know them as well."

"You forget that it was actually me who introduced Allegra to Tristan," said Sofia, waspishly, with a tinny note of spite in her voice. She had had designs on Tristan herself and when he had met her half-sister, the heiress to Estrella, he had transferred his affections, in one smooth move, without a backward glance. Sofia ground her teeth a little at the thought. It wasn't that she had ever been in love with Tristan, but she had thought that marrying him would solve her financial problems. Now it turned out that although he had inherited a grand old estate, his family was utterly penniless and the place was falling down around their ears, and he was himself hoping to marry advantageously. And of course, Allegra the heiress had fitted the bill. What was even more annoying was that he did seem to genuinely adore Allegra, with all her conventional English rose beauty and sweet disposition.

"Well of course you did," said Henrietta, remembering the circumstances that had first brought Tristan to Hampshire. "So of course, it will be nice for you to spend some time with them." This translated as they were a good social connection. Sofia sighed deeply, and suddenly a trip to Cornwall didn't seem such a good idea.

"So, that's all settled, you can drive Nat down in the trailer and bring the chestnut mare back. See what sort of possibilities Nat has as a three-day event horse for you in a few years."

Sofia smiled faintly. She didn't particularly want a barely broken in novice horse, she wanted another Gully, or possibly two or three other Gullies, she needed a string of brilliant horses if she was ever to get to the top. But she had to make the best of what was on offer and at least Henrietta acknowledged her ambitions, and showed signs of continuing to support her in them. She didn't mind taking Nat to

Cornwall, he was a big strong horse and she had helped Sarah break him in and at least it meant she would have something to ride. In a couple of years, no doubt Nat would be a good possibility. She just had to keep on agreeing to Henrietta's plans and hope she would get her big break soon. Sometimes she felt her face would crack with the amount of polite smiling she was doing.

Nat was loaded into the trailer a week later. Along with a mountain of tack, horse feed, supplements, rugs and all the paraphernalia that top-class, pampered horses needed. Sarah, the head girl, went with Sofia to help with the driving, then she was to get the train back from Penzance. Sofia had packed her riding clothes, but also some summer outfits, both casual and formalwear and a couple of bikinis. She planned to get to the beach at some stage and perhaps try surfing at St Ives.

They arrived at Treloar late in the afternoon. The sun was shining, and the gorse flowers lit up the moors like a golden blanket. Sofia was surprised, she remembered the landscape as dark and bleak and forbidding as it had been in the winter. It was rather beautiful down here she thought, a wild sort of abandoned beauty after the ordered green fields and woods in Hampshire. It reflected her own change of mood. The ocean glinted topaz blue in the distance. Scattered daffodils bobbed their heads up and down along the roadside.

Vanda had been looking out for them and came out onto the road as they roared up the hill. She was dressed in blue jeans and a bright red singlet top, her long blond hair in a thick plait hanging down her back. She opened the big farm yard gates so they could drive straight in and park. Sofia was a little surprised at how happy Vanda appeared to be to see them, she was smiling warmly, affectionately, and kissed her on both cheeks.

Nat came down the ramp looking unaffected by his long journey. He gazed around enquiringly. He was a big brown horse with no pretty, white markings but well conformed with an athletic body, a good length of neck, a flowing topline, and intelligent, kind, dark eyes. One of his best points was his calm temperament which belied his youth.

"Perhaps you should put all your gear in that smaller barn, which is the one that Beatrice used as a tack room?" suggested Vanda eyeing the mountain of equipment a little quizzically. She had never really got to grips with the whole materialistic horse thing. She was a minimalist by nature.

Nat was put in the loose box that was next to the one where Clovelly had been previously spending every night. He looked around with calm interest.

"We've got to remember that on no account does Nat go in a field with the red bitch," said Sofia, her voice rising a little as she remembered the horror of Alfie's injury from the mare. She still blamed Clovelly.

"Of course," said Sarah, putting her arm around Sofia's shoulders. She was really the kindest and most considerate of people. If she hadn't been so nice, it would have been extremely irritating.

"Look there are four fields. In Beatrice's time, the bottom one was used for schooling and jumping, but we can turn one of them out there. Then there's the small field above it, with the shelter." She waved her arm down the hill, towards the village and the sea. "And over there are two large hill fields, and even some trees, there is quite good grazing as well.

"You've got a marvellous set-up here," said Sarah. "All this grazing and somewhere flat to school, you are lucky,"

Sofia said nothing. She hated herself for being so mean-spirited but it seemed that every relative she had was an heiress and it was never going to be her. She pushed down her resentment, determined not to let it show. She made an effort to chip in with a cheery remark.

"Yes, it's great up here, and miles and miles of moorland to ride."

"Yes, I like it," said Vanda noncommittally. She didn't like to talk about her inheritance. They stood there in silence watching Nat who was pulling a few strands of hay out of his haynet.

"Perhaps we'll put him out tomorrow, once he settles," said Sarah.

44

"He seems pretty settled now," remarked Sofia, feeling unreasonably defiant, wanting to contradict.

Then Vanda made a move for the door and the two others drifted after her. "I'll show you your rooms if you'd like to bring up your bags," she said.

The farm house was large. There were four good sized bedrooms upstairs, a large living room, a smaller study, and a kitchen family area downstairs. Sofia was given the best guest bedroom, the wide window looking up to the moor, with a view of the weird tumble of rocks on the top of the hill. She could even crane her head to the left and see the line of blue sea shimmering seductively on the horizon about half a mile away. She threw her bags in the corner and went back downstairs. She noted that all the surfaces were clean, the curtains washed and ironed and the carpets spotless. The rooms were reassuringly spacious and airy, the furniture light painted wood with a trendy distressed effect. Vanda was in the kitchen preparing afternoon tea and Sofia remembered what a wonderful cook her cousin was.

"We can have tea on the terrace outside," said Vanda, piling large orange scones onto a plate with little pots of thick cream and dark red plum jam.

"Pumpkin scones," said Sofia, thinking this was going to be much better than the diet-conscious meals served at Estrella.

"Yes, and I prefer English Breakfast tea," said Vanda.

"Sounds good to me," said Sofia.

Sarah came down the stairs and into the room.

"Oh, I do envy you," she said. "The most wonderful views, it reminds me of summer holidays when I was young." Outside on the terrace, they relaxed a little now that all the polite things had been said.

"What was it like? When that old woman died?" asked Sofia a little brutally, not remembering her name.

"Well it was strange, I've never seen a dead body before," said Vanda. "And it happened much sooner than we had thought. There was a funeral and everyone from the village came, and we threw her ashes out to sea, over the cliff."

"It sounds like something out of a movie," said Sarah, not quite sure what the polite response might be.

The conversation drifted on to safer topics. The sun dipped below the horizon. Sofia went to check on Nat, giving him his evening feed. She stayed down in the barn sorting through the gear, putting it in more ordered piles. She felt restless now she was here. It was the weird feeling of shifting from one world, the ordered luxury and respectability of Hampshire to Cornwall where she had felt such an exile on her previous visit. The others called her back for a last cup of tea and then they all drifted off to bed.

Chapter Eight

Golden early morning light streamed through the orange-checked, gingham curtains in Sofia's bedroom. She opened her eyes and thought, 'I'm in Cornwall'. She had been woken by the sound of a powerful car roaring up the road outside the open window. It must be either a tourist, or a delivery. It pulled to a halt with a scattering of gravel. There was the bang of a door slamming.

Do you know a Christie?" Vanda called up the stairs a few minutes later. "He is asking to see you!"

Vanda was intrigued. She rather liked the look of this man, he didn't seem to be a silly, little, rich boy like Tristan, who was known locally as the Lord of the Manor. He even appeared to be quite intelligent, his grey eyes taking everything in.

"Would you like a coffee?" she asked him, while they waited for Sofia to stumble downstairs.

"Yes, thank you, black no sugar." Sofia joined them. She had taken the time to brush out her long black tresses and etch in her eyebrows, and a touch of blush on her high cheekbones. She took the coffee that Vanda offered her and stood there sipping it - her unfriendly green eyes glinting over the edge of the mug.

"Hello Sofia," he said evenly, registering her lack of welcome.

"What do you want?" she asked directly, not bothering with polite nothing-conversation. Sofia didn't like Christie at all, even more so since she had found out that his father was one of the richest men in England. She didn't suppose that Vanda, with her purported socialist beliefs, would approve of him when she knew about his moneyed background.

"You have a lovely place here," said Christie politely.

"Thank you," said Vanda pleasantly. "I like it. The seclusion."

She could see that Sofia didn't like this man, no doubt he had offended her in some way in the past. She sighed, really her cousin was hard to please.

"So, what do you want?" Sofia repeated her question.

"I came to see you about the chestnut mare, Clovelly Princess," he replied.

"Oh," said Sofia, raising one eyebrow haughtily. "What about her?"

"Well - I was wondering if you were thinking of selling her? I would like to buy her."

Sofia was flummoxed. It had never occurred to her that Christie might have any interest in Clovelly.

"Why do you want to buy her?" she countered, curiosity overcoming her dislike.

"I was thinking that I might train her up, for some steeplechase races."

"Oh, that's right, you work in the jump racing stable, in Wiltshire."

"Yes, I also ride in the races myself and I've always liked the look of her. I was going to offer to buy her from Tristan before, and then he organised the swap with you." He was obviously making an enormous effort to maintain his calm and keep the annoyance out of his voice.

"So how much do you think she's worth?" asked Sofia, deciding to place the ball firmly in his court. Besides, she had no real idea about the valuation of horses, and certainly not potential steeplechasers.

"Well I thought perhaps £8000?" he said a little hesitantly, he didn't like Sofia, he had her pegged as a heartless, brainless, little fortune-hunter.

"Ten thousand and she's yours," said Sofia, wildly plucking the figure out of the air.

He looked at her with increased dislike and there was an awkward pause, tension hanging in the air.

"All right, ten thousand, give me your bank details and I'll transfer the money today and I'll pick her up this afternoon." He disliked her so much he just wanted it settled so he didn't have to speak to her again.

"All right," said Sofia, not knowing what to say or how to feel. She had expected him to haggle. She wondered if she should shake his hand, but she really didn't want any physical contact. Then it dawned on her, £10,000 sliding into her bank account and she would be rid of the horrible bitch of a mare that she felt had been hanging around her neck like an ugly rotting albatross.

Christie left with only the most peremptory farewell.

"Well that was rather surprising," said Vanda, watching Sofia curiously. She was burning to ask her cousin about this Christie, how she knew him, but Sofia slid her eyes around and hurried outside, she was in no mood to discuss anyone from Penmar Hall. She walked across the yard squinting against the early slanting summer light. Inside the barn it was cool and dim. Nat looked across at her with mild curiosity, obviously hoping for his breakfast, which at Estrella would have been served up an hour ago. Clovelly was still down in the field.

"So, that horrid bitch is off to Christie and racing, whatever that means!" burst out Sofia. Nat raised his head a little. He was alert to the vicious tone in Sofia's voice, somehow it offended his gentle easy-going manner.

Sofia went over to the next barn where the feed was stored. She consulted the copy of the stable diary that Sarah had prepared for her so she could continue to record Nat's routine. After his feed, he could go out in the far field. It would be good for him to have a bit of a rest after his journey yesterday and a new and interesting field, well away from the lethal hoofs and teeth of Clovelly.

*****

49

Clovelly Princess was picked up that afternoon. Sofia checked her bank and the money had been deposited. It was all over in about ten minutes. The mare walked onto the trailer in a way that suggested that she was glad to be out of there. Afterwards Sofia felt light and richer. Perhaps a little empty but most of all relief.

"Mrs Bowles rang up and she's coming over to talk to us about the camp," said Vanda.

"Well I suppose it's best to know what is involved," said Sofia vaguely, really it was the last thing she wanted to do.

"She'll be here later this afternoon," said Vanda. "So, don't go disappearing on that horse, you really need to talk to her. I'm going to do the catering but the horse side of things is up to you. Sarah has gone tramping over the moors, she plans to walk to the cliffs and look at the sea."

Mrs Bowles arrived in a dilapidated old Austin that looked like it should have been put on the scrapheap many years ago. She was wearing a muddy brown skirt with an uneven hemline and the ubiquitous hand-knitted cardigan with leather buttons, and sensible laced black shoes. Her face hung in folds and wrinkles, right down to a triple chin that wobbled as she moved. Sofia found it impossible to hide her grimace of distaste.

"How do you do?" said the old lady brusquely, offering her hand for a very firm handshake.

She looked into Sofia's face and hurrumphed as if she was displeased, by what she saw.

"So," said Vanda, taking control. "Please, sit down Mrs Bowles and we can have afternoon tea."

She had brought out Beatrice's best delphinium-blue flower-patterned tea service, with a matching teapot and milk in a little jug, and white sugar in a dainty bowl. Mrs Bowles slurped her tea and Sofia felt sick at the sound, she would rather be dead than turn into this ghastly type of ancient wreck.

"So perhaps you can tell us how many pony clubbers are signed up for the camp?" asked Vanda, a pen poised over a lined pad.

"We've got the three Tregonning boys, a drippy girl with a horrible Dartmoor, Jenny who is off the council estate and will be unmounted, unless she can cadge a pony from somewhere, Xanthe who is a ghastly little social climber, Maddie who is carrot-haired, but an amazing rider with a broken-down old mare."

"So that makes three boys, and three mounted girls, one girl unmounted," said Vanda, wondering a little at this unflattering description of the pony clubbers. It seemed as if the old harridan didn't even like young people.

"Oh yes, and Izzie Littleton," said Mrs Bowles.

"Izzie, of course," said Sofia. "I've got an idea, what if Izzie could lend Beau to the child without a pony. I'm assuming she's still got him, she said she could never bear to sell him."

"Well you can always ask," said Mrs Bowles.

"What about Zane, you know Dane's son, who lives down at the headland," asked Vanda.

"You mean those Gypsies!" exclaimed Mrs Bowles.

"Yes, I do," said Vanda firmly, looking the old woman directly in the eye.

"Has he got a pony?" asked Sofia, as usual impervious to the subtler social signals.

"I think so, I saw him riding the other day," said Vanda.

"Well I suppose, if he wants to and he'll have to pay," sniffed Mrs Bowles.

"At least that would be another boy," said Sofia in matter of fact tones. "So, tell me Mrs Bowles, what do you think we should do? Instruction? Jumping?"

"Allegra, Sofia's sister said that she would be willing to do a dressage masterclass on her mare," said Vanda.

"Really, I didn't know that!" exclaimed Sofia, feeling a bit put out that Vanda was talking to her half-sister. "But of course, that would be good, fill up some of the time."

"Yes, that's fine, although I'm not sure whether they'll really be up to dressage," said Mrs Bowles.

"Well dressage is really only training with a fancy French name," said Sofia. "I suppose they all love jumping, and perhaps some fun, gymkhana games."

"Yes, all that sort of thing," said Mrs Bowles.

"So, what exactly are you planning to do?" asked Sofia as politely as she could. "Do you want to do some of the instruction?"

"No! I thought I'd leave that up to you. Your cousin says that you're an expert," said Mrs Bowles with another juicy sniff.

"Well I'll certainly give it my best shot," said Sofia, thinking what an annoying, prickly, old woman she was.

"I'll organise all the food and I'm happy to pay for it, as my contribution," said Vanda.

"But where will they sleep?" asked Sofia, hoping that she wasn't going to have to give up her bedroom, or even worse, share it.

"Well they'll have tents, the Tregonning boys said they'll organise that, set up on that flat area along the stream," said Mrs Bowles.

"And we can do the schooling in the bottom field," said Vanda.

"Perhaps I can set up a few cross-country jumps for them on the hill," said Sofia.

"Yes, that sounds just the thing," said Mrs Bowles. "I remember now you won the open competition at the Winters' hunter trials last winter on that very plain brown gelding." At this insult of her beloved, now-dead Alfie Sofia nearly spat at the hateful old woman.

"So, it sounds like there is a range of ability, let me get this straight, the girl Madeline is a very good rider, Xanthe, what is she like?" asked Vanda quickly, trying to keep them all calm.

"She thinks she's brilliant, she has expensive ponies but I wouldn't rate her much compared to Madeline. That girl Essie is apparently hopeless. I don't know that Jenny off the council estate can ride much at all. Obviously, Izzie Littleton is competent enough, well you know her, don't you?" said Mrs Bowles.

"And the boys, the Tregonnings, what are their names?" asked Vanda.

"Tom is the youngest and he has a very useful little dun pony, a mare called Goldie, he jumps and does very well at games. Dominic has a flashy grey mare and he's certainly capable enough, and the eldest boy, Nick is also a good rider, he has a rather plain, but workman-like cob," replied Mrs Bowles.

"The other thing I need to know about is dietary requirements," said Vanda. "Vegetarians, allergies?

"I have no idea," said Mrs Bowles disapprovingly, as if such things as vegetarians were ridiculous. "Here's a list of their phone numbers if you would like to ring them. And I thought if you compiled a list of things they should bring, that might make it easier."

"Perhaps we can have a meeting beforehand so we can all get to know each other, and answer any questions they have," suggested Vanda.

"Yes, if you like, I think I'll leave it to you then," said Mrs Bowles, getting up and preparing to leave.

"I'll be in touch later." She left abruptly.

Vanda and Sofia looked at each other quizzically.

"Well I suppose it's good that she's going to leave it up to us, not boss us around about every detail, the less I see of that gruesome old hag the better!" said Sofia.

"Yes, I'm sure we'll manage. It's only a weekend, it shouldn't be a problem," said Vanda.

Sarah was pulling her boots off in the kitchen. She had been out walking on the moor all afternoon.

"Oh, I have had a wonderful time," she said, her cheeks rosy from the fresh outdoor wind, "I went all the way down to the cliffs, this is the most magnificent place."

"Well while you've been off enjoying yourself," said Sofia. "We've been dealing with old Mrs Bowles, she's like something out the 1950s."

"Well, I'll be sad to be going back to Hampshire tomorrow," said Sarah. "You're going to have a wonderful time here in the weeks ahead you make the most of it Sofia."

Chapter Nine

Sarah was booked on the train the next morning but she jumped out of bed early, thinking that she might fit in a ride up on the moor. Although there was no-one to show her the way she thought she would just follow the path that she had walked the day before. For a moment, she wished she was staying here with Sofia through the summer, but she had her work cut out back at Estrella, breaking in the rest of the young horses.

Creeping down the stairs in order not to wake the others, she let herself out the back door. She gave Nat a small feed and while he was eating, she tacked him up. It looked like it was going to be another picture-perfect day. She led him out into the yard and he stood calmly for her to mount then he stepped out obediently.

Sofia got up and went downstairs an hour later. She was surprised when she read Sarah's note that she had taken Nat out. Of course, Sarah had every right to ride him but Sofia had planned to go out on a long ride herself. She wasn't sure what she would do now, perhaps go up to St Ives and rent a surfboard and see if she could teach herself to ride the waves, it was probably much the same as horse riding. Vanda was in the study reading and she came out and declared she was going over to Truro to visit her mother.

"Would you like to come too, to meet your aunt?" she asked.

"No, I don't really feel up to it today, perhaps another day," said Sofia as tactfully as she could. She felt like she had already fallen down so far in the world, getting acquainted with a putative aunt who sounded like she was in the category of the very dregs of society would be just too much.

"I'll drop Sarah off, she is going to catch the eleven o'clock train."

"Right-oh. I'll just hang out round here, do some more work on planning the camp." This was, of course, just a polite excuse.

The farm house was very quiet after Sarah and Vanda had left. Unaccountably, Sofia felt a little abandoned. Now she had the whole day to herself and absolutely nothing to do. She led Nat down to the bottom field and let him go, securely shutting the gate. He wandered off quite happily to graze. She went and sat by the stream dangling her feet in the clear running water. Then she heard the dull thud of unshod hoofs coming up the path. She squinted down the hill and saw two ponies coming around the corner at a brisk trot. They were unusual in that one was pink, the other blue.

"Hello there!" she called, standing up.

"Oh hello!" squeaked the young girl on the strawberry roan.

"What pretty ponies!" exclaimed Sofia, looking them over carefully. The smaller red roan gelding was well put together, although his head was too large and coarse for a show pony, his shoulder a little straight for a comfortable ride. He looked quiet and reliable. The blue roan mare was a different kettle of fish. She was light boned with a flashy black mane and tail, perhaps half-Arab. The tall thin boy was not wearing a crash cap and his long stringy black hair hung around his face. But he rode exceedingly well, sitting easily on the mare who was sidling and skittering.

"She looks like a handful," said Sofia.

"She's all right, just needs to get used to me," replied Zane with a touch of surliness in his voice. He had enough of his father in him to resent criticism, especially from a woman with a posh accent. But Sofia was feeling so lonely that any company was preferable to none.

"Would you like to come inside for a cool drink, you could tie the ponies up in the yard."

"Oh, that would be lovely," said Jenny quickly. This was a dream come true, she had wanted to befriend the people up at Treloar for so long. "I'm coming up here for the Goonhilly camp at the end of the summer."

"Oh yes," replied Sofia, "I'm helping out. Tell me your name?"

"Well I'm Jenny Salmon, and this is Zane."

"Oh, I understood that you were to be unmounted?" queried Sofia.

"Well I'm not sure, you see I'm just riding Berry for Zane's father, he bought them at a sale and he's planning on selling him as a child's pony, so I don't know what will happen by then."

"Yes, and Vanda suggested that you might like to come, as well Zane."

Zane looked uncomfortable and didn't reply.

"Come on, you can tie the ponies up in the yard, come inside for a drink," said Sofia.

They tied the reins of the bridles to baling twine which was looped through two rings that were attached to the solid granite wall of the barn.

"Come inside, there's some home-made lemonade in the fridge. My cousin, Vanda, makes it, very refreshing."

It was quiet and cool inside the farm house after the dazzling midday heat outside. Jenny and Zane were looking around curiously. They had never been inside the yard before, let alone invited into the house. Jenny was amazed at how beautiful it was. Everything looked so clean and fresh with gingham checked fabrics on the chairs and the curtains, so different to the tired, dull. stained velvet upholstery of the furniture in her family's living room.

"About the pony club camp, do you know what sort of things we'll be doing?" she asked.

"Well there'll be instruction, you know schooling, riding around at the walk, trot, canter and then trotting over small jumps and so on, depending on the level of the riders. And then of course jumping, and some gymkhana games. And perhaps that's where you can help me," suggested Sofia. "Do you know any of the pony club members who are coming?"

"There are the Tregonning boys," said Jenny. "They live over Sennen way, the eldest, he's grown up really, Nick he's left school and helps run the dairy and he's got this horse that they use to round up the cows, thickset and very plain, called Bob. Then there's the middle boy, he's a bit older than me, fourteen, Dominic, well really he's just called Dom, and they say he's a marvellous artist, he draws pictures and stuff. He has a very beautiful, grey mare called Guinevere, and Tom, he's a year younger than me. He has a really cute, nippy, little pony called Goldie. They win every gymkhana event, Goldie is absolutely fab at bending and potato races and things."

"All right, that's the three Tregonning boys then, Nick, Dominic and Tom, got that. Apparently, there's a girl with a little Dartmoor pony."

"Oh yes that's Essie, she's my friend. Her pony is called Pablo and he's quite small, probably too small for her as she's growin' very fast. We've been tryin' to train him but it's hard work, he's not very obedient, I've been riding 'im a bit but I can't make him trot, he only walks and when you try and turn 'im he just turns his head and not his body." That certainly fits the description thought Sofia to herself, suppressing a smile.

"So how long have you been riding yourself Jenny?" asked Sofia, wondering how she was going to cope instructing children of such disparate abilities.

"Well truthfully I've only just learned to trot and canter on Berry. He's the most marvellous pony, so kind, but I'm afraid he's going to sell very quickly when Dane advertises 'im."

"Yes, well a good child's pony is hard to get, he certainly looks very sweet. So, I guess you haven't had a lot of experience yet. I think the other two riders booked in are called Xanthe and Madeline, do you know them at all?"

Jenny screwed up her face, thinking hard.

"I know of them a bit but I've never really talked to 'em. They're from up St Ives way. They say Madeline, well she's called Maddie, is a fantastic rider. Xanthe is meant to be a bit stuck-up."

"Right," said Sofia. "Have you jumped at all yet Jenny?" she asked, changing the subject.

"Well no, I've just been getting used to cantering, but I would love to jump," said Jenny, her bright blue eyes sparkling. Sofia felt an unusual kindness towards her, she's just like me loving horses. But then I had all the advantages, and couldn't imagine what it would be like to be a poor kid in a tiny village dreaming of ponies and not having one of her own.

"Why don't we make some arrangements for you to come up and we can do some work with Berry, and you can start by trotting over poles and things like that. I need a bit of practice at instructing."

"So, you're not exactly a teacher," said Zane evenly.

"Well no, I mean I've had a lot of coaching, and I went to pony club myself for years, now I guess I have to look at it from another point of view."

"Do you mean if I come up here you can give me lessons? Oh, you can't imagine how wonderful that would be," said Jenny. "And what horses do you have? I noticed that big brown horse in the bottom field."

"Yes, that's Nat, he belongs to my step-mother, he's only just been broken in."

"He's very handsome," said Jenny. "You must be awfully good to break in horses and train them." Sofia smiled at her. This young girl certainly had a gift for saying the right thing. She went to the pantry and found a cake tin with half a saffron cake in it.

"Look would you like a slice of this, I believe it is some sort of Cornish cake."

"Yes, that's saffron cake, it's awfully good, they make it in St Just you know," replied Jenny. Even Zane was looking at little enthusiastic.

"Well I've never tried it but let's have a slice each," said Sofia cutting up three very generous pieces of the yellow cake thickly studded with dried fruit.

They sat in silence munching. Sofia did like the taste of it.

"The other thing that we're doing is my sister, Allegra, she's really into dressage. She's bringing up her mare, Skydancer and is doing what is called a masterclass. That is to say, one of the kids will be selected to ride the mare and she'll instruct them. Skydancer is highly educated in the art of dressage."

"So, do you do dressage as well?" asked Jenny.

"Well yes, of course, but I do three-day eventing, you know where you do dressage on the first day, cross-country on the second and show jumping on the third. I must admit I prefer the jumping."

"Oh, that sounds just wonderful," breathed Jenny in ecstasy. Then anxious to include Zane in the conversation she gestured towards him proudly. "You know Zane is going to be a jockey in horse races in a few years."

"I think we should get back," said Zane. "Dad will be wondering where we've got to."

"Oh, of course," said Jenny. They fairly rushed out the door, untied the ponies and led them back down to the stream path.

"Well make sure you come back and we can do some training, teach you to jump," said Sofia a little forlornly, thinking that she had fallen so far down the social scale that she was reduced to trying to make friends with local kids. She watched them ride back down the path. She looked at Nat who was quietly grazing in the field and wondered what she was going to do with herself down here for all the weeks ahead, just riding one horse was not going to fill in enough time. Really, she should be riding up to ten advanced horses a day like the top riders.

She turned to go back up the house, it was still early afternoon. She would think positive. She decided to ring Max Winters and ask him if she could go around his cross-country course tomorrow, perhaps he would invite her over to help with his horses, it would be great if she could somehow wangle herself a ride in some competitions. She suddenly felt distinctly friendless, and she had no desire to socialise with Allegra and Tristan, being the third wheel in that relationship was a very unappealing thought. She went back into the house and put the kettle on, to make herself a coffee. Pulling out her mobile she rang Max's number.

"Oh, hello Max, this is Sofia Pendleton."

"Oh hello, it's good to hear from you again. I had heard you went back to Hampshire.

"Yes, well I did go home, but I'm back in Cornwall now. I'm staying with my cousin Vanda, up at Treloar."

"Yes, I went to Beatrice's funeral and heard that Vanda Peregrine had inherited the property."

"I've brought down one of Henrietta's young horses, getting him used to being out and about. I wondered if I might bring him over to your place and give him a spin around your cross- country course?"

"Certainly, you can," said Max smoothly.

"What about on Wednesday morning, would that suit you?"

They made a plan and Sofia hung up. At least it was something to do. What she hated most was inactivity.

Chapter Ten

Sofia had been to Max's place before last winter, when she had competed at the hunter trials on Alfie and her other horse who was now owned by Izzie Littleton. Alfie had won and Del was fourth. She couldn't bear to even remember it now that Alfie was dead. She shut it out of her mind and concentrated on the present, 'the past is a foreign country', she muttered to herself. It was some random phrase she had heard on television but it seemed to fit the current situation. She was to concentrate on training Nat, it was a worthy objective. She wasn't that keen on Max Winters. He loved to gossip. There was a malicious edge to his tongue.

She drove over the moor down the Penzance by-pass and towards Helston. When she saw the sign "Celestial Equestrian Centre, she turned off. She had arrived half an hour early. She surveyed the stable yard. It was not as grand as Estrella. The boxes looked smaller and there were no fancy flower pots or illuminated statue. She jumped out the four-wheel drive and one of the young girl grooms, buxom and blonde, came over to help her.

"Max is just inside. You are to go around with him and Maddie."

"Maddie?" queried Sofia.

"She's Max's latest project. He thinks she's got a great future."

"Fair enough," said Sofia.

Max walked out of the house wearing too tight breeches and expensive long brown leather boots, swishing his whip against his boots in a rather pointless, macho manner.

"Hello Max," said Sofia, trying to inject some genuine friendliness into her voice, but there was just something about him that irked her.

Maddie turned out to be very young, perhaps only fifteen and painfully shy when introduced. She was of very unprepossessing appearance with carroty red hair and large pale brown freckles sprinkled all over her face. Her redeeming feature was a pair of enormous blue-grey eyes, but with very fair eyelashes and no eyebrows. She certainly isn't making the best of herself thought Sofia. But she had the longest skinniest legs, which were certainly good for riding.

Maddie swung up lightly and settled like a feather in the saddle. Max mounted after climbing onto the mounting block. They walked out towards the start of the cross-country course.

"Max told me that you're organising the pony club camp, I'm coming with my own mare Cinnie," she said confidingly as they rode out of the stable yard. "It was such a shame that Mrs Leigh died she was a lovely person."

"I never met her," said Sofia, "But you must be Madeline, I remember now, so you like to be called Maddie."

"Yes, I'd heard about that camp," said Max leaning over so he could listen in to their conversation.

"Now young Maddie," said Max patronisingly. "Remember what I told you yesterday, knees and ankles soft, keep the centre of gravity back, don't throw your body forward on take-off. For a sloping fence you go strong and fast and let the horse set himself up. For a table fence or a combination of fences, you have to tell the horse that there is more to this fence than first meets the eye, go down through the gears, but maintain the momentum."

"Yes Max, I've been thinking about everything you taught me yesterday," said Maddie meekly. Sofia smiled to herself. She liked this young girl, not only did she ride like an angel with the softest hands she'd ever seen, but she knew how to handle egotistical old men.

They trotted around a sloping field in large sweeping circles. Nat behaved in his usual impeccable way, he was a little excited but it made no difference to his levels of obedience. Sarah had really done a superb job breaking him in.

"I like that horse," said Max approvingly. "Have you any idea what Henrietta is planning to do with him?"

"Well I guess eventing, that's what he was bred for," replied Sofia shortly. What did he think the horse was going to do?

"Have you started wearing an inflatable jacket?" asked Max.

"No, not really. Henrietta bought me one but I haven't used it. I went on this course years ago, how to roll when you fall off, and when the jacket inflates you can't roll away."

"Well I guess its swings and roundabouts," said Max knowingly.

"Let's go, a nice easy fence to start them out," said Max riding towards a very low tree trunk. Sofia concentrated on Nat, he wasn't very experienced at jumping at all. She followed about three horses' lengths behind Max and they cantered on over the log with Nat barely breaking his stride.

"Good boy," she said encouragingly, running her hand lightly down his neck. Maddie followed behind her. Max swung around and headed for another tree trunk jump that was slightly higher. Again, Nat jumped over it as if he had been doing it for years.

"Have you tried any drop fences with him?" asked Max.

"No, not yet, I guess today is as good a time as any," said Sofia. They trotted on towards the edge of the quarry that was in the next field, jumping a low hedge along the way.

"These natural jumps are much the best for training," said Sofia to Maddie who rode up beside her.

"He probably likes being with the other horses as well," said Maddie.

They got to the edge of the quarry.

"There's a gentler slope down over there," said Max pointing. "You go Maddie, give her a lead, and remember that you have to keep two-thirds of the horse in front of you, and perhaps even more going downhill. If you swing forward then you'll end up tipping onto their ears."

"Yes Max," said Maddie submissively.

Nat noticed that Maddie's horse had disappeared in front of him. He went up to the edge and stopped, looking over the lip of the quarry in mild astonishment. Sofia sat on him quietly and let him look, then gently she pushed him on and he did an enormous leap. She was ready for it, hooking her lower leg in front of the girth and they landed safely.

"Oh, that was good," said Maddie.

"Come on, come back up Maddie, I want to see you take him over this side!" shouted Max.

Sofia pulled Nat up and patted him gently. They turned to watch the other horses jump the two-metre drop. Sofia remembered how she had jumped it with Alfie at the open event and he had made a gallant leap that had given them several lengths and they had picked up speed across the floor of the valley. She didn't want to remember, it was the past, she had to look to the future.

"So, what has happened with that horse Gullivers Travels?" asked Max, and Sofia could hear the malicious curiosity in his voice. Whatever she told him would be embellished and then relayed around the eventing circuit.

"He's just resting for a while," she replied carefully. "While I'm down here and then I expect we'll be competing in October, November, I'm not sure yet."

Well he's certainly a horse that's got all the buttons but I have heard that there were some soundness issues a few years ago" said Max. Sofia's heart sank, it had occurred to her before that Gully might have a history of lameness but she hadn't wanted to even entertain this unwelcome thought.

They rode off at a canter and came to a set of three elements, arrowheads set at different angles, perhaps six or seven strides between each of them.

"Off you go Maddie, circle around first then that one, that one, and that one. Point him just off centre towards the skinny end and take it at ninety degrees to the imaginary centre line down through the middle of the arrowhead."

"Right you are," shouted Maddie back. Her big grey horse flicked its ears when it heard her voice. She turned left in a wide arc and approached the jump and Max shouted again.

"Don't lose the outside shoulder around the corner or he'll drift! Don't bend your wrists, keep them in a straight line. Steer with your legs, try not to use your reins so much."

Maddie certainly handled it well, the big grey horse didn't look easy to ride. Sofia decided not to bother with the arrowheads, they demanded too much technical expertise, way beyond the capabilities of Nat at this stage. She was pleased with the way he had tackled the drop fence and she would pop him over a few more hedges on the way back to the stables. Perhaps in the past, she would have pushed him and over-faced him, but now she was very conscious that she had to do the right thing.

Back at the stables Max and Maddie had two more horses saddled up and ready for them to take out. Sofia watched them ride off and loaded Nat back into the trailer. She was a little disappointed that Max hadn't suggested that she take one of his other horses out. Perhaps he didn't really think she was a good enough rider. On the other hand, he might have tried instructing her the way he did Maddie and that would have been awful. She'd just drive home and have a nice cup of tea and Vanda would be back from Truro and they could relax. Perhaps she should even get her textbooks out and do some studying for the BHS exam.

Chapter Eleven

After Zane and Jenny had said goodbye to Sofia they had ridden back down the stream and around the outside of the village past Essie's cottage. Jenny felt guilty that since she had been riding Berry she had not got around to trying to help with Pablo and she wanted to be friendly and call by. Essie's cottage had very neat flower beds, interspersed with little squares of green lawn. Essie ran down the garden path when she saw them.

Oh Jenny, Zane, how wonderful that you've come, and your ponies they look so pretty, such striking colours."

"This is Berry and this is Blue. You know Zane, don't you?"

"Oh yes, kind of, hello, hello. I don't suppose you could help me catch Pablo, I thought perhaps I could come riding with you."

"Yes, I think we have time, don't we Zane?" asked Jenny. He nodded.

"If we take the ponies down to his field, he'll probably come up to us," said Zane.

"Essie! Essie!" called her mother. "The most wonderful thing we're to go to see a pony for you!" She came running out of the house, a neat old-fashioned flowered apron flapping around her waist. "Oh, it's you, Jenny, I didn't know you were here. What extraordinarily coloured ponies!"

"What do you mean we're going to see a pony for me?" asked Essie.

"Well," for a moment her mother paused, as if embarrassed. She appeared not to want to speak in front of the other children. "I was talking to a friend at work and she's told me about a pony for sale, up near St Ives, it belongs to a girl called Xanthe, what an odd name? But anyway, we're to go up and see it this afternoon."

"You didn't tell me you were going to buy me another pony?" said Essie. "But that's wonderful, and Jenny can come with me, she can help us to decide, perhaps she could try it first. And Zane of course as well, if he wants to," she added uncertainly.

Belinda pursed her lips, she had been rather hoping that Jenny not being around lately had meant the end of what she saw as an unsuitable friendship, but it would be too awkward to say that Jenny couldn't come.

"Of course, Jenny can come, but she's riding this other pony?"

"It's all right, I'll lead him home, you go, Jen, you'll like that to go and see another pony and have a ride," said Zane. Jenny looked at him, then looked at Essie.

"Well if you're sure," she said sliding out of the saddle and taking the reins over Berry's head she handed them to Zane. He rode off immediately as if to make sure she didn't change her mind. Berry trotted obediently beside Blue, they were both eager to get back to the camp.

"So, what is this pony like?" asked Jenny, thinking what marvellous luck it was for Essie. First, her mother buys her one pony that is no good, so her mother buys her another. "What are you going to do with Pablo?"

"Well we'll sell him of course," said Belinda a little impatiently. "There's no point in having two ponies." Essie's mother had no idea that ponies and horses hated being by themselves and longed for the company of another equine, or at least some sort of other animal.

"No, I suppose not," said Jenny, thinking if she had her way, she would have half a dozen ponies.

Essie got in the front passenger seat and Jenny slid into the back seat of Belinda's neat little car. They went up the winding coast road and turned off just before they got to St Ives. It was only half a mile along a narrow tarmac road, heading inland and they came to Xanthe's house. It was a large five-bedroom bungalow with a very smart set of stables built out the back. Four loose-boxes with white walls and dark-blue painted doors, and there were extra matching sheds, probably one for tack, another for feed. When they pulled up in the driveway Xanthe came out. She was dressed in very expensive clean pale blue jodhpurs, a crisp white shirt, and shiny bright electric-blue boots.

"Hello, you must be Xanthe," said Belinda, impressed, and just a little uncomfortable, by the smart set up and the way that this girl was dressed. Xanthe had blonde hair, neatly pulled back in a ponytail, all corkscrew curls and small hard blue eyes, candy-pink cheeks, and a pursed rosebud mouth. She looked rather like an old-fashioned china doll, thought Jenny.

"This is my daughter Essie, who has come to look at the pony," said Belinda gesturing towards her daughter. "And this is Jenny, she's from the village," she added dismissively. Xanthe smiled, turning up the corners of her little mouth, but the warmth of her welcome didn't reach her eyes. She knew that she was meant to be pleasant. Her mother had explained that if they got a good price for the pony then she could have a brand-new Prestige dressage saddle, so she was putting herself out to be pleasant. She barely glanced at Jenny who was wearing filthy scruffy jeans and a baggy old stained green t-shirt.

"My mother is inside, making some afternoon tea, would you like to come in," she said politely.

"Oh, how considerate, that would be lovely," said Belinda. "Perhaps you girls should take your shoes off," she said catching sight of a fluffy, light-cream, hall carpet. Xanthe looked at Jenny pointedly, thinking it wasn't just her boots that were going to mess up the house. Jenny sidled in, feeling hugely intimidated by the smart pretentiousness. Xanthe's mother came out into the hall. She matched the interior decoration perfectly, done up in a smart fitted beige skirt with a navy blue top and a discreet string of pearls, that were undoubtedly real. Her hair was coloured an improbable-ash blonde, carefully coiffed in an elaborate style as if she had just returned from the hairdressers. Her mouth was like a bud, the same shape as Xanthe's. Her fingernails were long and perfectly manicured, painted a frosty silver. The cruel distaste in her face was smoothed away by hypocrisy.

"Oh hello, Belinda, we spoke on the phone, how do you do?"

"How do you do?" said Belinda. "This is my daughter, Essie, and Jenny from the village."

"Come in, come in, I've just made a pot of tea and we've got sponge with jam and cream from Marks and Sparks." Her insincere laughter tinkled, as she turned on her heel and led them down the corridor.

They sat down in the dining room on rather hard and uncomfortable dark-grey chairs, grouped formally around an oval smoky-glass table. There was a pretentious ceremony of tea, sugar, and lemon presided over by Xanthe's mother. Despite the swirling atmosphere of insincere and artificial friendliness the cake was utterly delicious. Jenny had never tasted anything so fluffy with luscious cream and bright red strawberry jam, like mouthfuls of heaven.

"Do tell Essie about the pony," suggested Belinda. "She is rather excited at the prospect of seeing him." Jenny noticed how Essie's mother's accent had altered, she was speaking much more carefully in a posh sort of way.

"Yes, well Xanthe has been riding him for a number of years now, but she's shot up and rather outgrown him and she has a new horse, called Gemstone. Actually, Gemstone is a dressage horse, but Xanthe's planning to teach her to jump. So, you see her Boxer has to go. He is a frightfully good jumper and very nifty when it comes to gymkhana events."

"How big is he?" asked Essie.

"He's just under 14.2 hh, so he's ideal for the junior jumping competitions."

"What colour?" asked Essie.

"He's a lovely thick chocolate-brown colour with a creamy-white star on his forehead, rather a handsome chap."

Essie beamed at them. "He sounds wonderful I can't wait to see him."

"Well as soon as we've finished our tea Xanthe will take you out. She can jump him around the jumps that we've set up in our arena."

"You have your own arena?" squeaked Jenny.

"But of course, how else could Xanthe train the horses," said her mother dismissively.

It seemed to take forever, sipping tea and watching the mothers delicately nibbling their slices of sponge, which they ate with cake forks. But eventually Xanthe led them back out the front door and around a path to the stables. Essie ran over to Boxer, whose head was looking out over the stable door and patted him. Jenny stood back, she felt rather uneasy and her usual good-natured ebullience had drained away. Belinda kept saying she was 'from the village' as if it were a bad thing. She looked at the gelding and thought that he was not really handsome at all. His head was like a rectangle and although he was a lovely chocolatey-brown colour, his eyes were small and mean, rather like Xanthe's eyes. She had read it in a book from the library that when you go to view a pony for sale you had to make sure not to show too much enthusiasm. Obviously, Essie hadn't read that book.

"Oh, he is just beautiful, can I help you tack him up?" she asked.

Xanthe lead him out and tied him up to a ring embedded in the wall and put on a very attractive brown leather jumping saddle. Then there was a matching leather bridle with a flashy red and white browband, a ring snaffle and a rather complicated running martingale and breastplate. Jenny stood back and tried to assess his conformation. Besides the large rectangular head, he had a very short thick neck, a straight shoulder, and rather disproportionately short legs. But on the plus side, as far as she could tell, he had extremely powerful shiny hindquarters. He did look very strong and presumably that's what made him a good jumper, but really, he looked more like a harness pony.

Xanthe mounted in the stable yard and rode into the field where the arena was as long as a dressage arena but twice as wide, with a thick sand covering. It was bordered by a very neat, white-painted, wooden fence. She trotted around a couple of times and Jenny noticed how she niggled the pony's sides with her blunt spurs and flapped his neck with her whip, pushing him on and at the same time pulling him in.

71

He trotted smartly but without elegance, then he began to canter jerkily as if he was a clumsy marionette on a string at a puppet show. Xanthe's stirrup leathers were very short, and her reins tight and she did this weird posting thing as he cantered, as if she was rising up and down at the trot. Jenny remembered seeing some American girls doing it on You Tube on the internet.

After about five minutes of warmup, she turned the gelding and cantered him slowly towards a line of three jumps set up in the middle of the arena. He cleared each of them, but it didn't look smooth or fluid. He cantered jerkily up to each jump, came almost to a dead stop and then cat jumped, with the strangest action, going straight up in the air and then twisting over the top pole, tucking up his hind feet. But undoubtedly, he cleared each of them. This performance was repeated twice more, then Xanthe pushed him into a hand gallop, and finally he seemed to extend his neck a little, but he still looked much too short in front. They pulled up in a flourishing dramatic halt on the far side of the arena, his head in the air, his mouth open.

"Oh well done Xanthe!" called her mother, clapping her hands as if it was a performance at a circus. Jenny wondered whether they were meant to clap as well.

"I must say that was very impressive," said Belinda.

"Oh, I love him, he's so well trained, not at all like Pablo," said Essie. Jenny said nothing. No-one would have been interested in her opinion anyway.

"Now it is Essie's turn to ride," said Xanthe, smirking a little as she rode back. She pulled the stirrups up two holes and held him while Essie mounted. "You have to make sure you keep him on a firm rein," said Xanthe in a know-it-all voice. "It's called being collected."

Essie tentatively squeezed him with her legs.

"Do push him on a little more firmly, he has to know that you're the boss," said Xanthe. Essie walked him around the arena. She looked very nervous and Boxer looked very bored. "Ok, that's fine, now push him into a trot, don't forget to tighten up your reins, and use the whip."

Essie obeyed the instructions as best she could. Boxer trotted and she rose up and down in time to his stride.

"Oh, you are doing well," said Belinda, hoping that her daughter was making a good impression on these people, they certainly seemed to know what they were doing.

"Now canter!" said Xanthe. Essie found it difficult to get him to break out of his rough trot but eventually down the long side she gave him sufficient ragged aids that he grudgingly obeyed and broke into a jerky canter. Essie looked very uncomfortable bouncing in the saddle.

"It's just that she's not used to him. Pablo, her present pony, is very small," said Belinda apologetically. She didn't add that they had never even been able to get Pablo to trot, let alone canter. Essie pulled him back to a trot quite easily and rode back towards them.

"Oh, he is lovely and ever so obedient," she said puffing a little.

"So, what do you think?" asked Belinda.

"Oh, he is wonderful I would like to have him," said Essie.

"Well that's good," said Belinda as Xanthe and her mother smiled warmly with utter insincerity. "Her father is going to pay for him you know so if you could just give me your bank details, he can transfer the money. But I'm not sure how to get him back to our place."

"Don't worry about that at all, we'll be pleased to bring him over to you," said Xanthe's mother. No-one suggested that Jenny had a ride.

"Perhaps you should just walk him around the arena a couple of times to cool him down then you can unsaddle him and put him back in the stable."

"You know we don't have a stable," said Belinda worriedly. "Will he be all right in a field?"

"Is there a shelter?" asked Xanthe.

"Yes, there is a small three-sided shelter where there is his water and a rack for hay."

"Well, as long as you rug him. I'll include his rugs so you won't have to buy any, he's got a summer fly rug and a weather-proof winter rug that you can use as well. What about tack? Would you like to purchase his, or do you have your own?"

Belinda looked a little confused. "I'm not sure whether Pablo's saddle would fit him, perhaps we should buy yours as well, it's in very good condition."

"Well we'll charge you just an extra £350 for that," said Xanthe as if bestowing a huge favour on them. Jenny wondered how much they were paying for Boxer but obviously they had discussed that on the phone before they came over. She was glad that no-one had asked her opinion as she didn't really like him. Although she thought all horses and ponies, in general, were wonderful there seemed something a little sour about this rather ugly horse and she wondered how Essie would get on once they got him home. If they turned him out with Pablo then perhaps the naughty little Dartmoor would teach him all the bad habits he had been getting away with.

They drove back soon after that and Essie was chattering away, her thin pale face animated with excitement, her rather long pointy nose jumping up and down, her hands fluttering.

"Oh, thank goodness I'm going to have a decent pony to ride at the camp and we must advertise Pablo. Oh, if only we had an arena, I know it would make all the difference."

"We're not going to be able to stretch to that," said Belinda. "But perhaps your father might consider getting us a trailer, although of course this car is not nearly big or powerful enough to pull a trailer and I'm not sure that I could manage it."

"Well there is a truck that takes people to shows and perhaps Xanthe will take us. You know she has invited me over to visit next week. She is so nice, don't you think?" Essie chattered on without waiting

74

for an answer. "I just love her hair, so curly and blonde and she is an absolutely wonderful rider."

Jenny sat in the back staring out the window. She hoped that Zane had managed to lead Berry back to the camp. She suddenly felt hugely fond of the little strawberry gelding, he had such a sweet nature and she was sure that his rather bouncy short-striding canter was better to sit to than the strange jerky stride of old Boxhead, as she nicknamed Essie's new pony. She wished beyond anything that her mother would suddenly announce they were buying her a pony and then Berry could be hers. Although, of course, their backyard was not suitable for a pony. She wondered how much Dane would want for him, but whatever his price there was no way that she would ever be able to buy him.

Belinda offered to drop Jenny back at her house but she said it wasn't necessary. When they got back, she said goodbye and decided to walk down to the headland to see Berry. She felt depressed at the way things were panning out for Essie. It wasn't that she begrudged her friend a new pony, it was wonderful for her, but it made Jenny realise just how hopeless was her own situation.

It took about half an hour to get to the camp. The three ponies and the big stallion were tethered on the far side of the valley, where there was fresh green grass growing in the gully. Zane and his father were sitting in the shade of the caravan sipping mugs of tea.

"Hello, you two!" she called cheerily, thinking how much nicer it was here compared to the rigid cleanliness and modernity of Xanthe's house.

"Do you want a mug of tea?" asked Zane. As usual, Dane said nothing, but Jenny was getting used to his silence now, it was just his way. She sat down and drank her tea with them. Zane was looking a little uncomfortable.

"I'm real sorry Jen, but we've some real bad news, it looks like Berry is being sold. There's a girl Melanie coming to ride him tomorrow. It does seem like a really good home." Jenny looked at him, her blue eyes blank with despair. She knew it had had to happen but not this soon. She felt a silent scream building inside her. It was like someone had kicked her in the stomach and she found it hard to breathe. Essie was to get a new pony and she was to lose the one she had. She hung her head so the others wouldn't see how she felt.

"Look you're welcome to ride Blue, it's just that she's not that quiet yet, I'm not sure whether you'd be able to manage her," said Zane sympathetically.

"It's all right, I knew that he had to be sold, you told me from the beginning, it's just a bit sad that's all. I didn't think it would happen this quickly. Look I have to go," she said jumping to her feet and stumbling away. Zane watched her walk up the valley towards the village.

"It doesn't seem fair Dad, she wants a pony so much," he said.

"Life isn't fair Zane, the sooner you get used to that the better," said Dane staring moodily into the distance. "Don't worry, she's strong and if she wants it bad enough it will come to her in the end."

If Jenny had heard his opinion, she wouldn't have agreed with him. It was as if the gods were taunting her with the beautiful little Berry who had basically taught her to ride. Now he was to go to some horrid child called Melanie and again she would be back to going up the stream to give apples to Fred. She wouldn't have minded trying Blue but she was scary and there had been a number of times when Zane had almost fallen off and he was the best rider she had ever seen. Perhaps not quite the best, that was Sofia. Now she wouldn't be able to go up and get jumping lessons after all. In one day, everything had been snatched away from her, she was drowning in darkness.

Chapter Twelve

Jenny went up to Essie's house the next day when Xanthe's mother delivered Boxer. He was led down the field and introduced to the mischievous little Pablo.

"I hope he doesn't teach him any bad habits," said Essie worriedly. "Although he'll be going tomorrow morning. Mummy rang up Penzance Riding School, and they're coming to collect him." Jenny felt deflated, that meant she wouldn't be able to ride him with Essie on Boxer, all her chances were vanishing into thin air.

"Are you going to ride Boxer today?" she asked, trying to sound cheerful, thinking there was just a chance she might be offered a ride.

"Oh, not today," said Xanthe's mother disapprovingly. "He needs to get settled in." Now the deal was done she was in a hurry to get out of there. The warmth of her insincere politeness had almost evaporated.

"We're going into Truro later," said Essie. "To buy me some more riding clothes." She said it in such a way that Jenny knew she wasn't to be invited.

"Well I've got to get home," said Jenny. "See you later." She trudged off. It was obvious that Essie was dismissing her, seduced by the ghastly, but glamorous Xanthe. She went back to her own house, but there was nothing to do. The school holidays stretched before her like a desolate wasteland. She thought about a spoilt little brat called Melanie, probably riding Berry right at this moment.

*****

Bright sunshine washed across Jenny's pixie face as she lay in bed the next morning feeling as if she was going to dissolve into a grey puddle of grief. She just had to do something. She would go up and see Fred. She had neglected him in the last few weeks and he didn't deserve that.

The morning fresh air brushed her face as she jogged up the stream path. Small birds twittered in the ferns that leant over the edge of the water and she felt a bit happier. Sunshine always seemed to cheer her up. Fred must have sensed her coming and he was waiting at the gate. He eagerly crunched up the carrots she had brought him. Ponies didn't seem to bear grudges like humans.

After he had munched up all that she had he wandered off. She decided to go up to Treloar to see if Sofia was riding in the field. She rounded the curve of the stream path and saw the big brown horse circling in a springy collected canter, Sofia dressed in smart chequered jodhpurs and a trendy matching riding shirt. The gelding looked enormous, compared to Fred and Berry. Sofia's riding style seemed perfect to Jenny; it was as if she was a part of the horse, her back straight, the top of her head lifting to the sky, her heels down. After a while they stopped circling and Sofia looked over at Jenny.

"Hi there," she called and Jenny felt gratified at the warmth in her tone.

"Hi, he is going well," said Jenny, somewhat at a loss, desperately trying to think of something to say as Sofia rode over towards her.

"And how is that pretty little pink pony?" asked Sofia.

"He's being sold to a girl called Melanie," said Jenny dolefully.

"Oh," said Sofia. "That's not great, I'm sorry." She could empathise with the young girl's abject misery. She knew exactly how she felt. "I once had a wonderful horse and he was taken off me and given to another rider."

"Oh," said Jenny, thinking that at least Sofia had Nat now. It wasn't as if she was utterly horseless. Obviously, Sofia was reading her mind when she replied.

"You know this isn't my horse, he belongs to my step-mother, it's my job to train him." Again, Jenny thought of a world where one was paid to ride beautiful horses, it seemed utterly beyond her reach.

"Do you want to buy yourself a horse then?" Jenny piped up, suddenly inspired. "You know there's a horse sale up at Camborne tomorrow, you might find something there. That's where Zane's dad bought those three ponies."

"What type of horse sale?" asked Sofia quickly.

"Well, all sorts, I've never bin myself," said Jenny. "But there's some bargains, so they say."

"How far away is Camborne?"

"Just up the A30, not far."

"Well why don't we go?" suggested Sofia, the thrill of acquisition taking hold of her. She kept thinking she needed to get her own horse, so she had the right of possession. So that other people couldn't take them away from her. She had an extra £10,000 in the bank, which was probably enough to buy two dozen horses at the sale.

"Well what time does it start?" she asked.

"I dunno exactly, I guess about nine or ten in the morning, I can go down and find out and I'll come back up to tell ya," said Jenny.

"All right, then, I'll be here all day."

"I surely will," said Jenny, her face split with a grin.

She went back to the village to find her cousin, Damien and asked him about the sale, she knew that he had been there with their Great-Uncle Ted. "You know most of the horses go for meat?" he queried.

"Meat?" echoed Jenny, uncomprehendingly.

"Yeah dog food, you know, and sometimes processed meat that goes into ready to eat meals," he said nodding wisely. In fact, horses slaughtered for meat were shipped over to France, but Jenny didn't know that. She gulped, visions of beef burgers served up with toast and ketchup floated in front of her eyes, that was a standard meal in her house.

"Anyways it starts about ten," he said.

Jenny raced back up the stream. Sofia was still riding, trotting Nat over poles on the ground. She spotted Jenny standing at the gate and rode over.

"The sale is on at ten tomorrow morning," said Jenny breathlessly, hopping from one leg to another like a little bird.

"Cool. So, do you want to come with me?"

"Of course," said Jenny, steeling her soft heart against thoughts of horses being slaughtered for meat. "I can come up here in the morning, say I'm here around half eight, then we'll get there in plenty of time."

"No problem," said Sofia. "But let's go earlier I want to check out all the horses before the bidding, I don't want to miss my dream horse by being late." Jenny loved the way that Sofia talked. It was as if she was saying all the thoughts that filled her own mind. She wanted a dream horse, well at least a dream pony, but she had no money. Still helping her new heroine was second best.

Sofia decided to drive over to Penzance and withdraw a bundle of cash from the bank, she didn't know if they took debit cards at an auction. She had never bought a horse from a sale before and she was unsure of how it worked.

*****

That evening she and Vanda were sitting outside on the terrace sipping a rather good red wine. But there were dark clouds massing above them, a storm was coming. The sky was a strange brassy-green colour.

"Jenny and I are going to a horse sale tomorrow, up at Camborne," said Sofia.

"That should be fun," said Vanda politely, she was preoccupied, thinking about a new plan, to go abroad to teach English. Sofia poured them both another glass of wine. She was filled with hope, she would find some tremendous bargain - a superstar three-day event horse, ready trained for FEI events. At least things like that happened in pony books. Lightning started to stab the south-western sky and thick drops of rain splashed down on them. They ran inside, clutching their glasses and the bottle of wine then ate together in silence at the kitchen table.

"You really are the best cook," said Sofia when she had finished her tuna and red pepper pasta salad, flavoured with fresh parsley and basil from the herb patch.

"Thanks," said Vanda.

After dinner Sofia went upstairs. She stood by the window looking up at the carn, it was a dark hulk against the skyline. The rain was drumming against the window. Hopefully it would be fine again tomorrow. She lay on the bed and tried to visualise the horse that she might buy at the sale. She kept seeing Alfie. He had been over 17 hh and the kindest and bravest horse she had ever known. She had to think of another horse, conjure up an alternative vision. There must be another special horse out there, waiting for her.

It had stopped raining when she was woken by her alarm the next morning. She jumped up and went to the window to look at the weather. The moor looked different, everything gleamed, newly-washed after the torrential rain in the night. There were gulls soaring, screeching in the sky. She craned her neck to the left and she could see the glint of the sea in the distance. Something momentous was going to happen today, she could feel it.

Jenny turned up early. Suddenly the world looked hopeful, the unexpected was possible. There was something about the idea of horse sales that made her heart beat faster. All those ponies and horses waiting for a new home. If only she had some money. Within minutes, she and Sofia were rocketing down the dirt road then turned through the village and headed over the moor.

They got there early, more than an hour before the bidding was due to start. Sofia felt her dreams dissolving, she had never been to such a depressing place. It was down a backstreet. There was mud and puddles everywhere, the makeshift yards were leaning, the horses looked dull-eyed, with hollow flanks and rough, staring coats. Each horse had a round sticker with a number stuck on its rump.

They walked up and down the lines sidling between men who were swearing and spitting, hanging over rails and forcing horses' mouths open, inspecting their teeth knowledgeably. There was the stench of fresh horse manure and stale tobacco and beer in the air. An occasional pony was in good condition, sleek, grass-fed, and bright eyed. But the majority were bony, tired, with sunken backbones. A shrill whinny rang out and the other horses would answer. Uncertainty, fear, anxiety permeated the atmosphere.

Jenny took it all in through wide eyes. Sometimes a horse would be hauled out of the yard and run up and down, chased and walloped, and shouted at. The air was still cool but the bright sun overhead promised heat later in the day. In total, there were perhaps fifty horses and ponies to go under the hammer. There was a roped off area which constituted a makeshift sale ring. On one side, there was a wooden platform, on which would stand the auctioneer and his clerk. There was an old dilapidated caravan where you could buy coffee or tea in plastic cups, a collection of rather grubby sticky buns and jam donuts sitting on a plate.

"Well I guess we look at them in number order," said Sofia, a little uncertainly, she felt a horrible anti-climax. She couldn't imagine finding anything here that would be any good. They were almost at the end of the last row when she saw the horse, this was the one, without a doubt. It was a gelding, at least 16.2 hh, perhaps 16.3 hh, grey, not washed and shiny but neither poor and skinny and certainly not covered in sores. Sofia approached and held out her hand and stroked his face. Then carefully she opened his mouth.

"He's an eight-year old, or about that" she said a little uncertainly. She wished Sarah was here she was very knowledgeable at calculating the age of a horse by looking at its teeth. "But why is such a handsome fella like you at a sale like this?" she asked her voice soft, crooning gently. She slipped through the rails and quietly ran her hand down his front legs that were cool and hard, just as they should be. She stroked his neck on the near side and then across his back to the hindquarters. He was well-built without being sturdy, perfect for a three-day eventer, speed, and power in ideal proportion. Trying not to hesitate nervously, she ran her hand down his near hind leg and picked up the hoof, perfect, not boxy, although he was not shod and definitely needed a trim. Lastly, she pressed on each side of his spine, where the saddle would go, checking that he didn't flinch. He stood there steadily.

"He's fab," squeaked Jenny.

"Not bad," said Sofia unable to hide the undercurrent of excitement in her voice. "Do you think they ride them into the ring?"

"I don't know," replied Jenny, "I never bin here before."

"The ring doesn't look big enough for horses to be ridden," said Sofia. "Why do you think a horse of this obvious quality is here at the sale?"

"Well perhaps he's a rogue, he did something wrong," suggested Jenny. "Or someone died and their relatives just sent him to a sale."

"Perhaps," said Sofia, looking around anxiously. "Let's walk on, don't want to look too interested." They hurried back to the beginning of the lines and then Jenny pointed at a pony. They stopped together and looked at her. It was a mare, very thin and narrow. She was a taffy colour with a stripy white blaze, but dark points on her legs and a black mane and tail. Her eyes were rolling back and forth, looking around anxiously, as if searching for a lost friend.

"She's pretty, the colour of treacle," said Jenny, squinting her eyes up to see the beauty in the little animal.

"Much too small," said Sofia dismissively.

Jenny said nothing, inside she was crying out, 'but she's the perfect size for me'. Sofia looked down at Jenny's little face, which was rapt with love, and suffered a rare moment of insight into the feelings of another person.

"Well, she is such a lovely colour," said Jenny, then shrugged her shoulders at the hopelessness of the situation. "Perhaps you could train her up a bit and then sell her on as a child's showjumper, make a profit," she said in a last-ditch attempt to make a case. But she was without hope.

"Could do, but I don't think I'm cut out to be a horse dealer," said Sofia off-handedly. "Come on let's go and stand by the ringside, we don't want to miss anything."

Jenny stood there silently, she felt like she was going to cry. Her mind was brimming over with the thought of the little golden mare. She was the perfect height for her and with the most beautiful soulful dark eyes. If only she had some money but all her savings had been blown paying for pony club membership to go to the camp. Anyway, at least they'd found a possible horse for Sofia, her idea of coming to the horse sale wasn't a complete waste of time. That big grey gelding looked classy, too classy for this place, perhaps there was something horribly wrong with him.

"Do we have to register to bid?" Sofia reluctantly asked the man next to her. He had a round florid face and three chins, his stomach bulging over his belt. He smelt of tobacco and stale beer and normally she would never have talked to such a creature.

"No, I don't think so, if you win the bid then they come and take your name," he replied in a thick Cornish accent. She wrinkled her delicate nostrils in distaste, he really did smell. Eventually the auctioneer appeared, with streaks of greasy hair plastered across his yellow-coloured scalp. He was flanked on both sides by clerks who had narrow sallow faces, wearing cheap shiny suits. Stepping up to the wooden box he announced the official beginning of the auction.

A fat, dirty man led the first horse into the ring. It was an ugly big brown cob, rough-coated with dried mud on his legs. He had a pronounced Roman nose and a loose pendulous lower lip with strange narrow dull flat eyes, and an uneven shambling gait. The auctioneer spoke in an almost unintelligible sing-song gabble, strings of numbers and words and Sofia found it almost impossible to understand what he was saying. There were only a couple of bidders and the gelding was knocked down at a few hundred pounds. This set the pattern for many of the ensuing horses, the bigger the horse the higher the bid.

"This is like a slave market," Jenny whispered, her eyes filling with tears. She was now utterly convinced that all the horses were going to the slaughter house.

"Don't be so emotional," said Sofia dismissively. She was impatient, waiting for the grey horse. Then Jenny saw the little golden pony mare being pulled into the ring. She was digging her hoofs in, not wanting to do as she was told. At least she is small thought Jenny in despair, there wasn't much meat on her, hopefully she wouldn't be suitable for the butchers.

"Oh no, oh no," said Jenny, beneath her breath. The bidding only got to a hundred and then Sofia raised her hand.

"£200!" she called out clearly in her posh, cut-glass accent that sounded so out of place here. A few of the rough men in the crowd swivelled around to look at her. The other bidder, a most unattractive man with a face deeply scarred with old acne, shook his head and turned away.

"Going, going, gone," said the auctioneer banging his gavel. Jenny gave a little shriek and leapt up into the air. Then she flung her arms around Sofia.

"Thank you, thank you, thank you, you've saved her." Sofia flinched away from the physical contact, she didn't say anything. She felt a little confused about her spontaneous altruistic response to the situation. It wasn't as if she was into animal rights. She rather looked down on all that 'caring' nonsense. She didn't know what to do with Jenny's exuberant display of joy.

"OK, OK," she said. "I'm sure I can do something with her, train her up and pass her on for a profit." Jenny felt deflated. Perhaps for a moment she had thought that Sofia was going to give her the beautiful little mare. But at least she wouldn't go for meat. That was the most important thing.

Sofia was getting frustrated, the grey horse was one of the last horses to come into the ring.

"Come on, let's go back to the yards and walk around for a bit." Jenny was wondering how they would pay for the little golden mare, surely they should go straight to the office.

"Shall you go and pay for the pony?" she asked, her voice squeaky with anxiety.

"No, if I buy the grey, then I'll pay for both of them at the same time," said Sofia, "I just want to have another look at him, make sure he really is what I think he is." She found herself muttering, she didn't want to broadcast her intentions to this hostile crowd of people. She didn't feel that she fitted in here. She could see people sneering at her. There was a shady looking character standing looking at the gelding when they got there and instantly Sofia recognised a potential rival bidder.

"Do you think we can take him out and trot him up and down?" she asked.

"He ain't got a groom, has he?" replied the man. "This ain't Ascot."

Sofia stood there looking at the horse intently. His legs looked straight and clean, no sign of scarring where he might have over-reached or brushed. He wasn't quite as tall as Nat and there was something about his broad forehead and small ears that reminded her of a pony, as if he had some Connemara in him. That dash of mountain and moorland blood was good, for an extra leg round a tight corner. Perhaps he had behavioural issues, but there had never been a horse that she couldn't ride.

She and Jenny drifted back to the ring. The endless parade of ugly, thin, scarred, unhappy-looking horses was depressing. Some of the crowd seemed to have dispersed and she hoped this would give her more of a chance to win the bidding for the grey. Finally, he was brought into the ring. She had positioned herself so she could see him coming down the alleyway and as far as she could see he had true straight movement, but it was difficult to tell. There was a bit of a stir amongst the crowd, he really did stand out, he was different to all the others that had come before. Sofia could feel her heart beating and her palms were sweaty. She was breathless. She just had to have this horse, no matter how much she paid!

Chapter Thirteen

Sofia had been determined to be strategic and hold back. Be cool, not display too much interest, she had told herself. Now, she found she couldn't play the game. She was desperate and suddenly it didn't seem to matter. She had the money, she would pay whatever it took. Jenny's exultation at the purchase of the little mare was contagious. They were both in the grip of a shining vision.

The auctioneer was babbling and it was hard to understand him. She thought she had heard him say, "Seven hundred, eight hundred, nine hundred".

She raised her arm and could feel cold sweat running down her side, and shouted, "£1200!" Her voice cut through the air and there was a moment of silence, everyone seemed to be looking at her. The auctioneer pointed his fat, greasy finger in her direction, his eyes shiny with greed.

"Twelve hundred to the little lady, now who can better that, a fine piece of horse flesh here, a winner!"

Sofia held her breath. It was as if her whole life depended on it.

"Twelve fifty!" shouted a sallow man on the other side of the ring.

"Fifteen hundred!" she countered, knowing that she was doing it all wrong, she should be upping the price by only fifty. But she just didn't care.

"Fifteen fifty!" shouted the man aggressively.

"£2000!" she called in desperation.

"Two thousand we have from the little lady," said the auctioneer, laughing as if it were a joke.

The dark-skinned man glared at her furiously but didn't bid again.

"And he goes to the little lady, going, going, gone. Well that's a bit of quality here in this sale yard," said the auctioneer and the thinning crowd guffawed maliciously.

"Yes!" Sofia hissed to herself, but suppressed the urge to shake her fist in the air as if she was galloping the victory round after winning a competition. By now, Jenny was dancing a little jig with excitement.

"You got him, you got him, you won, you won!" she shrilled. The two of them hurried over to the clerk to sort out the paperwork, suddenly afraid that if they didn't pay and claim their purchases, they might be whisked away by someone else.

There was no queue in the office and a lot of the horses had already been carted away. Sofia handed over a bundle of new notes. The woman in the office laboriously counted them, examining each £50 note suspiciously. Eventually, she wrote out two receipts and handed them over grudgingly.

"Thank you," said Sofia feeling annoyed at the woman's attitude, she didn't like any of the people in this awful place and the sooner they got out of here the better. They hurried down to the holding yards and then Sofia realised that they didn't have headcollars or lead ropes.

"Bloody hell!" she muttered cursing herself for her own stupidity and lack of planning. If only Sarah had been there, she would have organised the details like that. She handed the car keys to Jenny.

"Can you run over to the car and see if there are any headcollars in there, or even just ropes, bridles, anything, so we can lead them out."

Jenny took the keys and took off. She was determined she had to succeed in this mission, otherwise they would be stuck with no way to get the horses on the trailer and home to safety. She got to the four-wheel drive and pushed one of the buttons on the key ring but nothing happened, so she tried the other and thank heavens the doors unclicked. There was nothing on the back seat or on the floor, then she noticed a large headcollar and rope laying in the rear compartment underneath an old towel. But there was nothing for the pony mare. She wrenched open the door of the trailer and there was a piece of baling twine knotted and twisted around an empty haynet that was attached to a ring. She struggled with the knot, and eventually worked it loose. She rushed back and found Sofia looking annoyed.

"Here this is all I could find," she said gasping for breath. Sofia looked at the baling twine.

"Well we'll just have to manage, I want to get out of this place. Here you take the grey and for goodness sake don't let him go, and I'll deal with the mare."

She fashioned a rough halter with the baling twine and managed to lead her out. Luckily the pony seemed to realise that she was being taken to a better place and obligingly followed the big gelding.

"He has to go on the high side, on the right, to keep the balance right," said Sofia, "I'll hold both of them, if you can manage to get the ramp down." Jenny struggled with the fastenings and then it released, swishing on its hydraulics.

"You hang on to her and I'll lead him on, and then we'll use his lead rope to give us a bit more control over the mare," said Sofia, again wishing that Sarah was here to take charge. It was all these tiresome practical details that she found so difficult. The grey led on easily, as if he had been going on and off trailers all his life. Sofia swung the rear bar behind him and fastened it, then went in and untied the lead rope, it wasn't as if he was going anywhere. She took it and tied it around the mare's head like a halter but there was only a short end left to use as a lead.

The little mare didn't want to load. She pulled back stubbornly and Sofia only just managed to hold onto her. She was flummoxed, the horses at Estrella had all loaded and unloaded with no trouble, perfectly trained and civilised, she had no experience of this sort of thing.

90

"Come on sweetheart," said Jenny, trying to coax her in, patting her softly.

"Look it's no good trying to woo her with soft words."

She took hold of the mare and walked a few steps up onto the ramp. The little creature was not co-operating. Sofia resisted the urge to shout at her in a bad temper and kept the pressure on the lead, so she couldn't turn her head to left or right, nor step back. They stood there for nearly ten minutes, a test of patience and determination. Eventually the mare took one grudging step forward, and Sofia released the uncomfortable pressure on her head for a moment, as a reward. Then she took up the pressure again. This time the mare seemed to understand and it took only a few minutes before she took another step forward. Again, Sofia let the pressure go, and then took it up again. Eventually, she had her two front feet halfway up the tailboard, and her hindfeet still on the ground.

"Shall I come up behind her and try to push her in?" asked Jenny uncertainly, remembering a picture she had once seen.

"Not for the moment," said Sofia, "It could just distract her and she might run backwards, or kick you, if we had another rope, we could try using it as a breaching rope."

They stood there for another minute then the mare seemed to just give in, she scuttled up the ramp, almost knocking Sofia over.

"Shut the bar!" shouted Sofia holding on tight. Jenny stepped up and managed to secure the bar.

"You did it, you did it!" she called, "Thank God!"

"Come on let's get out of here I've had enough," said Sofia in relief. "So back to Treloar!" she said as she turned the key and the engine roared into life.

"Yes, with two fab horses," said Jenny. Sofia looked at her sideways with a slight smile.

"Would you like something to eat?"

"Oh yes please," said Jenny.

"Well we'll pull up at the next layby with a food van and get us some hamburgers, and two cokes, or whatever it is you want." Take-away food was something of a treat for Jenny and she grinned, this was turning out to be one of the most exciting and wonderful days of her life. About ten miles down the road they pulled over to get the food. The excitement of the sale had made them both feel tremendously hungry. Sofia gave a £20 note to Jenny and went back to check on the horses. It was hot inside the trailer and the mare was sweated up and shifting around uneasily.

"So, what happened to you?" Sofia said softly to the big grey running her fingers gently down his neck, which was long and elegant. He really did have the most beautiful large soulful eyes. Her mind was buzzing with plans. She needed to call a farrier to get his feet done, perhaps the vet to do a full check and some blood tests, even some x-rays. But really, she just wanted to ride him, once she was on his back, she would be able to feel it, whether he was what she thought he was. Jenny came skipping back with hamburgers, two cold cans of Coke, and a couple of chocolate bars.

"Come on let's eat while we drive, I want to get back to Treloar, we've got some horses to sort."

"We surely have," said Jenny happily, biting into her hamburger and munching.

It was mid-afternoon before they made it back. They drove the trailer into the farm yard and unloaded the horses.

"First, we need to wash them, I've got some sort of medicated shampoo somewhere in that trunk of oddments," said Sofia. "Perhaps you could go inside and put a few pots of water on to heat," she suggested to Jenny. "Oh, yes and we need to worm them."

"Before they go anywhere near Nat," said Vanda who had come down the back steps to see what they had bought. Jenny scurried around getting together things that they needed.

"So, what do you want to call the little mare?" Vanda asked Jenny.

"Well it's not up to me, but perhaps Treacle, she's the colour of treacle, like what my gran puts on her scones."

"Yes Treacle, that's a good name," said Vanda, helping her to carry one of the big pots of hot water outside. They mixed it up with the purple shampoo and dipped in large sponges. They started soaping them down.

"She's got some scurf and dirt in her coat. It's a long time since this little girl got any care and attention," Vanda said running her fingers over the gaunt haunches.

"She's got no condition on her at all," said Sofia, looking over. "Not like this fellow, he's in good nick."

"Why did you buy her?" asked Vanda curiously.

"Why not," replied Sofia carelessly. Jenny bent her head, rubbing with the sponge, she dared not hope that the mare had been bought for her to ride.

"What are you going to call the gelding?" asked Vanda, sensing the tension in the air.

"I hate thinking of names," said Sofia, "We've got no idea of what he must have been called before, or where he's been or what he's done."

"It's strange isn't it to think of a mysterious previous life," replied Vanda.

"I think I'll call him Rimmi," said Sofia, as if by naming him she could establish control over the situation. "Mr Rimmington." She had no idea where the name came from but it seemed to suit him. He was old enough and mature enough to merit a title of 'Mr'.

After they were washed, they were put in two of the partitioned stalls in the barn. Sofia went in and mixed up some feeds. She gave them oaten chaff, high-performance and balancer pellets.

93

"I think I'll put some diluted molasses in as well, just to give them an extra treat." The three of them stood there watching them eat. Rimmi tucked in hungrily, munching away industriously but Treacle was more tentative as if she wasn't quite sure.

"She's not very confident, is she," said Vanda, "As if she hasn't had some great experiences."

"She'll cheer up now, we'll look after her," said Sofia. "We can worm them tonight. That should help." After being washed, their coats slicked down it was easier to see their condition and conformation.

"I think she's a two," said Sofia, standing back and critically evaluating Treacle's condition. "Look her ribs are showing, and you can even see the bone structure on her shoulder."

"What do you mean a two?" asked Jenny, uncertainly.

"Well it's a form of body condition scoring, one is the worst, positively emaciated, and she could be worse."

"How high does it go?" asked Jenny.

"It goes up to nine, which is extremely fat. But generally, five is the best, perhaps four point five for a horse in work, or five point five for a riding horse at the end of a good summer. You can look it up on the internet, it's called the Henneke scale."

"Come on, let's leave them in peace, dinner time, would you like to come in and eat Jenny?" asked Vanda kindly.

"I suppose I should go back home."

"But do come up tomorrow morning, I'm going to ride Rimmi," said Sofia.

Jenny skipped down the stream path, she was overjoyed, she had been invited back, it seemed as if Sofia wanted her around, it was more than she had ever hoped for.

Chapter Fourteen

Sofia didn't sleep soundly that night, she was tossing and turning and half-dreaming about Rimmi. Together they would clear the most enormous of obstacles, gallop the fastest and win competitions. She felt as if she was floating on a cloud of hope, inspired by shimmering ambition, then she would plunge to the depths of fear – perhaps he was a crock and she had been deluded. She woke early, jumped out of bed, and went down to the kitchen to make herself a cup of coffee. She slipped out the back door and barely noticed the weather, the cloudless sky promised another hot summer day. Crossing the yard to the barn, she didn't even look at the purple heather and golden gorse which made a beautiful mosaic pattern on the slopes of the moor on the other side of the stream. She was too intent on seeing Rimmi.

Nat nickered when she opened the door, he seemed to be telling her that he liked the company of the other two horses. She was relieved when she saw that Rimmi and Treacle were still on their feet - alive. She looked Rimmi over carefully, making sure that she had not imagined his good looks and over-estimated his potential. But now, comparing him with Nat, he was just as good looking as she had first thought. She sipped her coffee.

"So, my mystery boy," she said to him gently, almost as if addressing a new lover. "You and I are going to have a great future together."

She went into the other barn to mix the feeds and returned with three buckets. Nat was, as usual, the perfect gentleman standing back to let her tip the feed into his tub. Rimmi, on the other hand, was pushing his nose in as soon as she started to tip the bucket. Sad little Treacle stood shivering in the back of the stable as if she didn't understand the meaning of feeding time.

"Don't worry little sweetheart, you'll be loving your feed as much as these two hungry horses soon. And I'll let you go to munch on some good Cornish grass. We'll soon fatten you up."

She left them eating and went back inside to make toast, so she wasn't riding on an empty stomach. Vanda was still in bed. Sofia decided that she'd use her general-purpose saddle and perhaps a running martingale and a cross-over noseband, so she would have a bit of extra control if she needed it. The gullet had been adjusted for Nat who was a little more solid, compared to Rimmi's back which was shaped more like that of a thoroughbred, but it would fit well enough. She would ring the farrier at eight o'clock and arrange for him to be shod, and also Treacle's feet to be trimmed. This morning she would just ride him in the lower field.

She led him down the laneway. She had decided to lunge him a little first, just to be on the safe side. To really see if his movement was straight, she needed a helper who could run him out so that she could stand behind and watch. But lunging would give her a chance to evaluate his action. She put the lunging headcollar on over the top of the bridle. He waved his head up and down and shook it from side to side.

"You're a funny old thing," said Sofia laughing. "Are you trying to tell me something?"

Then she shook out the length of the lunge rein and flicked the whip lightly. He had obviously been lunged before and she had no need to walk in a smaller circle herself, following him from behind with the whip to encourage him. He bounded forward and was trotting in a circle around her. His stride was long and low, but he shook his head impatiently.

"So, you like to go!" called Sofia. "That's okay, so do I".

She flicked the whip again and he cantered, his head was tucked in to his chest. He was a good-looking animal, with a smooth, muscular topline, sloping pasterns, a good length of neck which was set high on the shoulder, which would ensure an elegant head carriage when he was schooled to move more correctly, accepting the bit. For a big horse, he had a particularly beautiful head, broad across the forehead with small, neat ears. Sofia was feeling increasingly pleased with herself. She squashed down any niggling misgivings about how he had ended up at the sale. Perhaps his owner had died and the un-horsey relatives had not known how to divest themselves of a good quality horse.

After about five minutes lunging him to either side he hadn't exactly settled. He seemed very fussy around the head but Sofia was still half-dreaming of all the success they would enjoy together and she was often careless with details. Sarah would have noticed but Sofia was impatient, she wasn't going to put off riding him for another minute. She took off the lunging cavesson and led him forward, to prepare to mount.

He stood perfectly still while she swung herself into the saddle. She took up the reins just a little, with only the tiniest tension and gently closed her legs and he walked off. His head was rather overbent, perhaps he'd been ridden with a much more severe bit in the past and he had gotten into the habit of overbending to avoid the extra pressure. They walked around the perimeter of the field. Then she took up a firmer contact through his mouth and pushed him into a trot.

That's when the trouble began. He started to shake his head, yawing from side to side, seeming to hate the feeling of the bit in his mouth. He reefed his head down pulling the reins through her hands then he flung his head into the air and Sofia was caught off-guard. He nearly whacked her in the face. He could feel that she was off balance and he began to buck. All four feet were off the ground, twisting like a rodeo horse with his head between his legs. This was no exuberant lift of the hind feet to show high spirits. This was utter determination to rid himself of his rider.

Sofia had never experienced anything like the ferocity and expertise of this bucking. She tried to pull his head up but this seemed to drive him into an even greater frenzy and with the fourth twisting bone-shattering buck she was catapulted onto the ground. He kicked out towards her, narrowly missing her face, and took off galloping around the field. She was winded and couldn't catch her breath and the panic seemed to rise as she struggled to breathe. Nothing like this had ever happened to her before!

It was the worst of all luck that at that moment Allegra and Christie arrived. Of all the people in all the world that Sofia most hated being made a fool of in front of, it had to be these two. She staggered to her feet, still desperately trying to get her breath.

"Oh Sofia! Are you all right?" called out Allegra, in her kind caring voice, which of course, made it all the more humiliating.

Sofia swayed a little, her head felt like it had been banged with a big hammer.

"Here sit down again, shall we take you to the hospital?" asked Allegra.

Everything seemed fuzzy in front of her eyes but Sofia couldn't admit this, not to Allegra and Christie!

"Is Vanda up at the house?" she asked.

"Of course, shall we go and get her?" replied Allegra with just a tiny note of hurt in her voice, that Sofia should prefer her cousin to her sister.

"I'll catch the horse," said Christie.

This galvanised Sofia into action.

"No, he's my horse!" she said emphatically, and made a huge effort to stand up again. The field seemed to be tilting around her. But by now Vanda had come hurrying down.

"Sofia, let Christie catch the horse and I'm taking you up to the house, you need to lie down in the dark for a minute then we can decide what to do."

Sofia felt an overwhelming need to prove that she was fine. She had to get back on the horse. But the thought of being bucked off again sent a wave of nausea through her. She began to throw up, feeling utterly wretched.

"No, no, no. Let Christie handle it," Vanda insisted. Then Sofia capitulated and let herself be led up to the house. They got her to the sofa and she lay down in the cool dark living room and at that point surrendered to unconsciousness. As she slipped away, she could hear Allegra and Vanda discussing what to do in low tones in the kitchen.

Christie was down in the field with Rimmi. He and Allegra had seen the big grey in a bucking frenzy. They had seen that Sofia had stuck on for at least four fantastic, twisting bucks before being thrown. Rimmi allowed himself to be caught. Then Christie noticed the headshaking. He had an idea.

"There, there big chap, let's have a look." He slipped his thumb into the corner of Rimmi's lips and the horse opened his mouth. He ran his thumb across the bottom jaw, along the bars of the mouth where the bit sat. He thought he could feel ridges in the gum, but he couldn't be sure. He'd seen it before, entropic wolf teeth in the lower jar, the pain of the bit on the gum could send the quietest horse mad.

He led him up to the stable yard being careful not to put pressure on the bit. Then leaving the saddle on he replaced the bridle with a headcollar and again slipped his thumb into the corner of Rimmi's mouth. When he touched the gum it definitely produced a reaction. He thought he might try to ride him in the headcollar. Of course, Sofia hadn't given him permission but she looked like she didn't know what day it was, so he would take the risk.

He attached a rein on either side of the nose band of the headcollar and adjusted the stirrup length. He didn't have a hat but he was prepared to take the risk. Perhaps it was just to prove a point. It certainly wasn't to impress Sofia, who he continued to despise.

Rimmi followed him quietly, back down to the field. Christie was too experienced in the ways of horses to be taken in by the horse's apparent submission. If he really was a rogue, not just a horse in awful pain, then this would be part of his routine.

Christie jumped on his back lightly and sat there very still. Rimmi was flicking his ears around nervously. Then quietly Christie closed his legs on his sides and they walked forward. Rimmi shook his head a little, as if waiting for the pain, but then finding no metal bit in the bars of his mouth pressing on his tender gums he settled and relaxed a little. He trotted and cantered around the field several times.

"Well at least this time you've learnt that bucking off your rider doesn't mean that is the end of work for the day," said Christie, gently stroking the big grey's neck. He liked this horse but it would be rather awkward if he suggested to Sofia that he buy him. It just would not be 'the done thing'. He dismounted and led him back up to the stable. After unsaddling him he took him over to the wash bay and hosed him down. Then after scraping off the excess water with a sweat scraper he led him back down to the field and let him go so he could roll and relax. Then reluctantly Christie walked back up to the farm house.

"How is Sofia?" he asked Vanda who was in the kitchen.

"Allegra is going to drive her over to Treliske Hospital at Truro to get checked over, it looks like she's got some sort of concussion. She hit her head pretty hard, made a decent dent in her hat."

"I've put the gelding back in the field, I hope that is all right. I did actually ride him myself."

"You rode him!" exclaimed Vanda.

"Yes, I hope Sofia won't object, but I think I know what is wrong with him. It could be entropic wolf teeth."

"I'm not sure what that is," said Vanda. "Could you write it down and I'll make sure I give it to her when she is back."

"It is quite easy if it is the case, he can have them surgically removed."

"Well, I'm sure that will cheer her up," said Vanda.

Allegra came into the kitchen.

"She's come to now and agreed to let me take her to the hospital. I can drop you back to Penmar Hall on the way Christie."

"Well I can come with you if that would be helpful," said Christie reluctantly.

100

"That is kind of you to offer but really it's not necessary," said Allegra. "I'll ring you Vanda when we know what the doctors say, I've got your phone number."

Vanda and Allegra took Sofia's arms and led her out to the car. Sofia was x-rayed at the hospital and there was no skull fracture. The doctor told Allegra that she should take her home and put her to bed for a day or two. Sofia was uncharacteristically quiet and acquiescent. Allegra suggested that she should go back to Penmar Hall with her but Sofia resolutely refused. She might be feeling out of it but she didn't want to have to be beholden to the Littletons, she would much rather Vanda looked after her. So, Allegra drove her back to Treloar.

Later that night Vanda sat at the end of Sofia's bed and talked to her.

"Christie thinks that Rimmi might have entropic wolf teeth. I've googled it and it is a very simple procedure to have them removed, and he could be just fine."

Sofia was torn, on the one hand it was great news, but on the other she hated it that Christie should be involved. And he had seen her bucked off!

"He said you should get him scanned. I'm not sure whether they have that facility here, perhaps in Truro," said Vanda.

"I'll take him back to Estrella and he can be treated in Hampshire," said Sofia. "Can you ring Henrietta and also Sarah, and get her to make an appointment at the Equine Hospital. I would like to drive tomorrow but perhaps I should wait til the day after."

"Are you sure you'll be up to it, driving that far, on your own?" asked Vanda doubtfully.

"I'll do it," said Sofia determinedly, "But now I must sleep."

"Well then good night," said Vanda.

Chapter Fifteen

Sofia had to wait three days before she was well enough to drive back to Hampshire. She left early in the morning and managed the journey in seven hours. Rimmi traveled well, picking at his haynet during the journey. When she arrived one of the young grooms rushed out and helped her to unload him.

"I do like this new horse!" said the girl, who was called Angie.

"Yes, he is rather handsome, isn't he?" said Sofia. She kept her mouth shut about the bucking issue. She was on tenterhooks, desperate to get him to the Equine Hospital to have him scanned so they could confirm Christie's diagnosis. If only it was just an entropic wolf tooth then it could get cut out and within a week the problem might be totally solved. On the other hand, he had obviously mastered his bucking routine, perhaps he would continue out of habit, having learned that it meant he got unsaddled and didn't have to work. Perhaps there was another issue. She felt feverish with the uncertainty. It was as if her whole life hung in the balance. She had tried to reason with herself as she had driven up. There was always Gully but she knew that he might be constantly beset with unsoundness and he wasn't her horse. Rimmi was hers and no-one was going to take him away; it just had to work out.

After Rimmi was installed in a loosebox she rushed down to the office at the end of the stable block.

"Sarah!" she called, "I'm back. You did get that appointment, didn't you?"

"Sure," replied Sarah calmly. She was used to Sofia's tumultuous approach to life, everything was always so dramatic for her. "I've got you an appointment tomorrow at lunchtime, the receptionist said they could fit you in at one pm."

"Oh, that's fab! Thank you so much. Look come and see him, tell me what you think. This ghastly man, Christie, you remember him he bought Clovelly, well anyway he says that he thinks that it might be wolf teeth coming through, or even worse a bone spur. I can't feel anything, but if there's a chance it's that, then all will be well!" she announced, the words tumbling out, one after the other.

"Of course, I'll have a look, let's keep our fingers crossed!" Sarah was privately a little worried that this new horse, bought from some seedy horse sale in the back of beyond would be a confirmed rogue and that would be £2000 down the drain and even worse they would have to get rid of him. And again, Sofia would have to cope with another setback.

She followed Sofia down to the stable where Rimmi, unaware of the drama that was going on around him, was tucking into the superbly sweet meadow hay that all the horses at Estrella enjoyed. He looked around to see Sofia and Sarah opening the lower door, then he went back to greedily pulling the hay out of his haynet.

"Well he's certainly a good eater," said Sarah, casting her eye over him. "And he is a handsome chap as well, nice clean legs with plenty of bone, and such a pretty colour! I know you thought he was thoroughbred with perhaps a touch of Connemara, but I think he looks like an Irish Sport horse."

"Well that's possible," said Sofia thoughtfully. "Yes, when I saw him at the sale his quality stood out a mile, he's got class, especially compared to most of the broken-down wrecks there."

"So how did he end up being auctioned off? Perhaps he started bucking and they couldn't do anything with him," said Sarah stroking his neck softly her fingers running down his coat in a whispering caress, massaging him at the line where the shoulder joined his neck. "And Nat? How is he?"

"He's fine, obviously I left him in Cornwall, but don't worry this kid called Jenny is looking after them, so Vanda doesn't have too much to do. She's doing a course in Truro, teaching English or something. I did take Nat over to do Max Winter's cross-country course. Honestly! That man with his retinue of young girls, he's creepy!"

"Apparently, he was gorgeous when he was young, I guess it's hard for him to grow old," said Sarah laughing. "But I'm surprised you haven't asked about Gully, I would have thought that was your number one issue?"

"Of course, you said he was better, that's absolutely fab, but do you think he's going to break down again, I'm a bit scared about it?"

"I don't know, who can tell, but tomorrow morning before you go to the Equine Hospital for the scans you can ride him out with me. I'll take one of the other young ones that I've just broken in," said Sarah.

"That's a plan then," replied Sofia, "I suppose I'd better head up to the house and check in with Henrietta!"

Sofia felt ambivalent about her step-mother. She knew she could never compete with the golden child, Allegra, but she had to admit that Henrietta had been jolly decent to her after her father had deserted them all, and now she was totally dependent on her, not just for employment, but also the ride on Gully and even a roof over her head. She had to squash down any resentment and make sure she was very, very polite.

She made her way down the path to the backdoor and calling cheerily to the housekeeper.

"Mrs Pendleton is in her office, she is expecting you," said Mrs Matthews, looking up from cleaning out the kitchen cupboards. Henrietta liked her relationships with the staff to be formal, they all had to call her 'Mrs Pendleton' there was no first-names friendliness in this household.

Sofia set off down the long passageway, her feet padding on the thick pale carpet. The furnishings were sparse, walls painted neutral colours, furniture chosen with impeccable taste. It was as if loud noises were always muffled and she felt her anxiety levels rising.

The office door was ajar but she approached cautiously and tapped discreetly before she entered. The prospect of talking to Henrietta always reminded her of being summoned to the headteacher's office. There were no floral arrangements in here, no sweet scents to make it homely, austere black office furniture, gleaming surfaces, and stark-white walls. Henrietta always looked rather grim, her thin lips and the permanent crease down the middle of her forehead, gave her the air of a rather strict matron.

"Ah Sofia, we must talk, there's something that we need to discuss," said Henrietta, in sombre tones. "Please sit down."

Sofia stared at her. This didn't sound good, perhaps someone had died, or maybe Henrietta had lost all her money? So, if Allegra was no longer an heiress then Tristan would dump her - that would be a joke! Or perhaps it was about her father who had left with no forwarding address last February.

"Yes, I've been thinking about this a lot. I think you need a fresh start, I thought it might be a good idea for you to go away to Hartpury College, to study, you can take Gully and this new horse of course, or perhaps Nat, if you would rather. You could have another shot at your A levels and then go on to do some sort of course. I don't think studying by yourself to do your BHS exams is really working out. You might benefit from living in a community, with other students, like-minded young people, and they have some wonderful facilities there you know, that is the college that I was thinking of but of course you could choose another if you wanted."

"Go back to school?"

"Well why not, you just don't seem to have proper direction, you really need some structure and you could build up a network of contacts as that is what you'll need no matter in what direction your equestrian career goes."

Sofia started to think, slowly. She felt so muddled, perhaps she was still concussed and the long drive hadn't helped. Going to college sounded awful. She had hated school but Henrietta was talking about taking the horses. Now she had had a taste of working for a living, the prospect of going back to school seemed like an easier option.

"Look here's the prospectus, I did send in an application for you a week or so ago, on the off chance that you might agree to the plan but I didn't apply for you to join one of the three squads. I thought that might just be too much pressure and the deadline has passed. But there are so many opportunities for you to work on your riding there, absolutely top-level tuition and you can apply to join one of the squads next year. I don't want to rush you but there is some time pressure. I want you to think about it, but we'll have to go ahead rather quickly if you do want to go."

Henrietta knew that she was pressuring Sofia at this point and that it was possible that it would be too much for her. She should have done this years ago. It had just never occurred to her and Robert had always been so close to his elder daughter that he wouldn't have liked her to go away to school. Now, Henrietta hoped that living in a tightknit community of other horsey young people would do her the world of good, she needed to grow up and learn to get on with other people. And as wonderful as Sarah was, and the private coaching that she'd had - it wasn't up to the same standard as what she could get at Hartpury.

Sofia felt herself thrown into a maelstrom of doubt and uncertainty. Of course, she knew about Hartpury, there were events held there and she vaguely remembered a girl who had gone there after she had finished school, to study a degree or something. She didn't like the sound of A levels but at least there would be facilities, possibly even better than what she had here at Estrella.

"I suppose that would be good," said Sofia, trying to process it all. "I could take Gully and Rimmi, as long as he comes good." Being bucked off ignominiously in front of everyone would be a nightmare, but if he got over his bad behaviour, she would have two amazing horses to be going on with. And she realised that Henrietta was acting as if Nat was to be her future mount.

"Well think about it, but there is some time pressure so we need to make a decision quickly," said Henrietta.

Sofia stumbled down the corridor heading back to the stables. She always thought better on horseback. She might just take Gully out for a hack around the park and get everything straight in her brain.

The last golden rays of summer filtered through the hazy air. The wonderful galloping horse statue in the middle of the stable yard looked as if it was gilded, surrounded by tubs of brightly coloured summer flowers, tumbling yellows, reds and oranges. The stable doors were painted glossy British racing-green and the ground was swept clean.

"Sarah!" she called.

"I'm in here," replied Sarah from the stable office. She came out into the doorway.

"Oh Sarah, did you know what Henrietta was cooking up, to send me back to school?"

"Yes, she did mention something. But you know Hartpury is brilliant. It's absolutely perfect for you. Not to mention all those hot French and Italian boys who go there."

"I suppose so," said Sofia, hesitating.

Gully was happy to see them, whiffling and nickering.

"He is such a charming gentleman this horse," said Sarah. "And his leg really seems as good as new. I rode him this morning and he went very well, about thirty minutes in the school then just a gentle circuit around the park. I've not jumped him at all, nothing too strenuous."

Sofia felt much better. Sarah was always so wonderfully reassuring. She suddenly realised how much she depended on her, going away to school would be difficult.

"How long do you think you'll stay before you go back to Treloar?" asked Sarah.

"I don't know. The camp is on in just over two weeks. My first priority must be Rimmi, they say you can ride a horse about a week after the operation, that is if it is entropic wolf teeth. Of course, I have to go back for the camp but it's all set to go, we've done the preparations."

"Well let's hope it is entropic wolf teeth and not bone spurs, as they can be rather more problematic."

"Don't even suggest that, I'm pinning all my hopes that it can be fixed. Look, I think I'll lead Rimmi out into the park, let him stretch his legs after that long drive today. Give him a chance to graze a little. I don't think he's used to being stabled.

"Good idea," said Sarah.

*****

Sofia rode out Gully the next morning and he went brilliantly. After riding Nat who was coming on well, but was still a little unbalanced, a bit clumsy. It was amazing to get back on a well-trained horse who responded to the lightest touch and was schooled to a much more advanced level. His paces seemed totally smooth, not a sign of unsoundness, but she was determined to take it slowly - it wasn't worth him breaking down again. But she was mainly preoccupied with what would happen with Rimmi. She was on tenterhooks to get a diagnosis.

Sarah went with her to the Equine Hospital. Rimmi behaved himself well and stood quietly while they scanned him. Then they waited for what the vet had to say. In the end, it was the news that they had hoped for, entropic wolf teeth. The operative procedure was scheduled for the next day. Sofia was walking on air, puffed up and filled with hope. Then she began to fret again, what if his bucking had become a habit that would be very hard to break. She had found to her own embarrassment that she wasn't much good at sitting a bucking horse, it was something that she had never really experienced before.

She spent the week riding Gully and helping Sarah with the other just-broken young horses. She felt superstitious, if she worked hard then Rimmi would come right. She agreed with the plan to go to

108

Hartpury and went shopping with Henrietta for her kit and even went so far as to help with sewing on name tags - not something she had ever done before!

Then one week to the day after the operation she carefully put on a bitless bridle from out of the tack room, saddled up, and led him to the indoor arena. The surface was raked smooth and there was the subtle smell of cut grass floating in from the lawn outside. Sarah had come with her to help, just in case. This was the moment of truth, when they would know whether getting rid of the pain was going to solve the problem. She walked Rimmi around the arena first, leading him and letting him get used to his surroundings. He was calm and collected, as if this was part of his normal routine. Perhaps he had been schooled and educated and then started going crazy and his previous owners had just given up in despair and sent him to the sale without a warranty. Sarah held him when she eventually decided to mount.

There was a hush in the indoor arena. Pigeons were coo-ing in the trees outside and dappled light filtered in through the high-set glass panels.

"Walk on," said Sofia, gently closing her legs, wondering whether the bitless bridle was going to work. She'd never ridden in one before. Sarah walked with them and they made their way slowly around the perimeter of the arena.

"Okay, this is it, let's trot and canter, I've just got to know how he's going to behave," said Sofia in a rush. She took up more rein and pushed him on. He glided into a smooth trot, his head bent at the correct angle as if he'd been trotting around arenas for half his life. Sofia felt an urge to laugh out loud and shout and punch the air but she controlled herself. Now, she was going to canter and that would be the proof of the pudding.

He sprang forward and for a moment Sofia was very afraid that he was going to plunge his head down and begin bucking. She sat back a little, and took up stronger contact on the reins. At least in here the surface was softer for falling off.

His head lifted and he was cantering. It was like marshmallow, long and smooth, absolutely perfect, so easy to sit to. Sofia was filled with exaltation, 'this was the one'! It was like falling in love, that irrefutable feeling of rightness, when the universe is painted in brighter colours and everything seems to glow and nothing will ever go wrong. She knew then what she had believed from the beginning that this was the special horse. They said there were two, or if you were lucky three, very special horses in your life and she knew without doubt that Rimmi was one of them. And he was hers, no-one could take him away from her!

"Oh yes Sofia! He is rather wonderful isn't he!" shouted Sarah, watching them from the middle of the arena.

"Oh yes, he is the one!" she shouted, a smile stretching from one side of her face to the other.

So, Sofia could see the future, straight and perfect, to college with Gully and Rimmi. Nat back at Estrella being brought on by Sarah.

Back at Treloar, Jenny was also in love, but for her it was a type of unrequited hopeless love. The future held no certainty for her at all. Treacle was not her horse and as far as she could see she would go back to Hampshire with Sofia after the camp. Again, she would be left with no pony, and not even one to ride.

Chapter Sixteen

Jenny was up early on the first morning after Sofia had left for Hampshire. Vanda was going into Truro every day, doing a course to learn to teach English. The weather was truly summery, warm and filled with sunshine from dawn until dusk.

Jenny felt rather important to be left in charge. And it had all been arranged that she was to ride Beau at the camp. So, on the face of it, all was right with the world. But in typical human fashion, the more she had the more she wanted. There was no certainty in her future. She had some great chances but only for the holidays, then she would be back to visiting Fred every morning, and not even Pablo to ride.

Vanda was still in the kitchen when she entered the farm yard.

"Oh, hello Jenny, it's so good that you can come up and do the horses, I really don't have time and there's going to be homework every night with this course."

"I love looking after them," Jenny replied. "I promise I'll do everything right. I noticed that you've been lettin' them go in the far field at the moment."

"Yes, that bottom field is getting grazed down and with the camp in two weeks I thought we should let it grow a bit. Also, they've got a bit of shade under those trees by the boundary fence - to get out of the heat. You might want to put the fly rugs on them during the day, it's up to you."

"Okay, I'll muck out the stables, and I thought perhaps I could give the tack room a spring clean. I noticed that a lot of them old leather saddles are dusty, really they need to be cleaned, covered up."

"Oh, you're a treasure!" said Vanda. "I've been busy in the house sorting through Beatrice's study I haven't got round to the sheds yet. See what you can find, perhaps we can put some of the stuff up for sale on Ebay, it seems a waste. Of course, you can have anything that you like, as a reward for all your hard work."

111

"Oh, thank you - that's amazing," said Jenny, thinking that it was too ironic if she was given a saddle and bridle but had no pony to use it on. Still she had to be thankful, perhaps Sofia would leave Treacle behind and Vanda would let her keep her in the field when she went away.

Vanda drove off and Jenny was left alone. She took in the feeds that she had prepared carefully according to the notes that Sofia had left. Except, Treacle was given a handful of extra crushed barley, to try to fatten her up. Nat was, as ever, the gentleman when she tipped his feed in, standing back politely. Treacle was cowering in the corner, as if she was afraid someone was going to beat her.

"You poor baby, you've had a horrible time, but I promise I'll do everything to help you," said Jenny, gazing at the little mare. She was sure that when she gained condition, she would be totally beautiful. She left her alone to eat in peace. Treacle was too nervous to eat with someone watching her. It was as if everyone was a potential enemy.

Jenny went into the barn that served as a tack room. One half of the room had been swept clean and Sofia's gear was there, sacks of horse feed, a couple of bales of hay, and her saddles all neatly stacked with saddle covers. The other half of the barn was dusty and cobwebs were strung across the corners. There was a pole with at least half a dozen dusty old saddles sitting on it. She would spend the morning cleaning this place. First, pulling out all the saddles and gear into the yard and then scrubbing the floor, the walls and clean the windows. Then she would set to work cleaning up the tack. She felt happy. There was sure to be some good quality gear here and perhaps Vanda would let her have quite a bit of it, she could sell some and it could go into her pony fund. Perhaps it would be possible to raise enough money to buy Treacle. She had to keep hoping.

She went back and checked on Nat and Treacle. He had polished off his feed and Treacle had eaten most of hers. Nat could go out first. He was easy, lowering his head so she could slip on the headcollar and standing patiently while she struggled with the buckles. He looked pleased to be going out for the day and trotted off up the hill.

He certainly was a handsome horse, thought Jenny. Perhaps a little plain with no white markings but when he moved, he looked so impressive, his low stride sweeping over the ground. She imagined that he would be fast when he galloped.

Treacle was looking even more anxious, probably because she had been left alone, without the reassuring presence of Nat. Jenny went in and walked up to her quietly, trying not to hesitate, feeling that she had to show confidence so that Treacle would begin to trust her. She managed to get the headcollar on and led her outside into the sunshine. The mare looked even thinner in the bright light.

"Come on sweetheart," said Jenny. "You can go out in the field and eat as much as you can, you need to fatten up." She led her to the gate and let her go. Treacle sprang into a trot, heading towards Nat who was grazing at the top of the hill. Jenny went back to her cleaning operation, determined to have the tack room spick and span before Vanda came back this afternoon.

She worked all day, stopping only for lunch. Vanda had left her some sandwiches on the kitchen table and she poured herself a glass of home-made lemonade from the fridge. It had taken ages to drag all the gear out into the yard, and there had been spiders and filth everywhere. Then she got a bucket of hot water and splashing it around tried to clean the floor, but the water wouldn't drain away and she had spent ages scraping out the dirt. There was no way she was going to be able to clean all the old tack by the end of the day and it couldn't be left out all night. She would wipe off the worst of the dirt and then stack it back in the barn and keep on with the cleaning tomorrow. There were still the stables to be mucked out.

Finally, it was five o'clock and Vanda would be back soon. She went up to the field to bring the horses in. Nat was waiting near the gate and happily got led back to his stable, looking around expectantly for his dinner. She went back to the field and saw Treacle under the trees. She walked up to her and the little mare turned and looked at her with pricked ears.

"You recognise me," said Jenny thrilled. She went up and put on the headcollar.

"And you're not running away." She pulled her around and then impulsively, without thinking about it, she jumped on the little mare bareback. She sat there feeling the bony backbone.

"Come on," she said nudging her heels against her. "Just walk back to the gate, there's a good girl. I'm exhausted from cleaning all day and all you've done is eat grass."

Treacle walked sedately back to the gate.

"At least you do seem to be broken in," said Jenny sliding off her, realising that what she had done had been foolhardy, she wasn't wearing a hat, there was no-one around to rescue her and worst of all Sofia hadn't said she could ride the mare. On the other hand, she argued with herself, she hadn't said that she couldn't.

She put Treacle in the stable and started lugging the saddles back into the barn, stacking them on their pommels in the dry corner on a blanket spread on the ground. The biggest ones first. They were old fashioned with flat saddle flaps, and no knee pads. There was no mould on the leather and you could see that for a long time they had been well looked after. There were also three smaller saddles, one very straight cut, like a showing saddle and two others a little more forward cut, probably used for hunting in the olden days.

Vanda arrived back about six o'clock.

"Hi Jenny, did everything go all right?" she called as she climbed out of the old truck.

"Yep, everything was great," said Jenny, "I've started cleaning up but I didn't get it finished."

"Wow!" said Vanda, looking in the old barn, "I can see this is a big job, you know you don't have to do this, just looking after the horses is enough, to help me out."

"I like it," said Jenny breathlessly.

"Here's a cream bun for you," said Vanda, handing over a paper bag.

"Yum, my favourite," said Jenny.

114

"I suppose you should be getting back for your tea," said Vanda.

"No worries, I'll be up again tomorrow," said Jenny.

On the way home, she thought about riding Treacle. It had been fine, nothing had happened. She resolved that tomorrow she might try to ride her a little bit longer. Perhaps she could try some of the old tack on her, to see if it fitted, and just ride her round the yard a few times. She told herself that Sofia wouldn't mind. Sofia didn't seem to care about Treacle at all. In all the drama of Rimmi the little mare had been quite forgotten.

After dinner, Jenny was tired but just couldn't settle. She decided to walk over to Essie's place and see how she was going with Boxer.

"Oh, hello Jenny," said Essie, in a different type of voice, her small watery eyes squinting, the end of her nose quivering, when she opened the door.

"Hi," said Jenny, her sweet lets-be-friends smile painted on her face. "How's Boxer going?"

"Why, are you thinking you want a ride?" demanded Essie, her voice all bitchy.

"No, I was just being polite," said Jenny, confused and hurt. This Essie was completely different to the shy timid girl who had arrived in the village with the awful Pablo.

"My mother says that I mustn't let you ride Boxer, Xanthe says that it wouldn't be good for him."

"Oh," said Jenny. She felt a lump in her throat, as if she was going to cry. There was an awkward silence. "Are you looking forward to the camp?" she asked uncertainly.

"Well I suppose so, really it's just for kids but Xanthe is going."

"Nick Tregonning is not exactly a kid, nor is Izzie Littleton," said Jenny, a little indignantly.

"Izzie Littleton?"

115

"Yes, she's going to go with her horse Bright Fidelity, well really he's called Del," replied Jenny.

"Well I'll have to tell Xanthe. You know she's going to be riding the dressage horse in the masterclass."

"Really, I didn't know they'd made a decision on that," said Jenny.

"Well how would *you* know anyway," said Essie, with the emphasis on you.

Jenny shut her mouth. She wasn't going to tell Essie how she had been spending time with Sofia, who was a billion times better rider, and more beautiful, and a thousand times more posh than that wannabe Xanthe!

"Well I'll be off then," said Jenny in a small voice. She turned and walked away, feeling Essie's eyes boring into her back. She felt sick in the stomach, as if she had been kicked, remembering how in the past she had done everything she could to help Essie with Pablo. And if it hadn't been for her the other kids at school would have picked on Essie, made fun of her long gawky legs and her strange up-country accent.

"Ungrateful cow," she muttered. Conveniently forgetting that her motivation for befriending Essie had been solely to get to ride her pony. She really hoped that Xanthe wasn't going to be chosen for the masterclass. She also wondered how Boxer and Essie were really going. Essie was hardly the world's finest rider!

She comforted herself with the thought of riding Beau at the camp. That would be one in the eye for Essie and Xanthe. She could have told Essie, crowed a little to make herself look more important, but she wouldn't bother, much better to see the look on their faces when they saw her riding him. Tomorrow morning, she would go up and do some more work on the tack room and perhaps ride Treacle around the yard. She began to day dream, she would ride every day and get Treacle going so well that Sofia would be amazed and decide that she could keep her.

Chapter Seventeen

Jenny felt very excited. Today she was to ride Treacle. She would use one of the small saddles that she had found in the tack room the day before and search through the tangle of old leather straps, browbands, and reins and put together a bridle with a rubber snaffle. She had thought about it a lot in the night when she couldn't sleep and decided that Treacle would feel more calm and comfortable being ridden in the farm yard if Nat was still in the stable

Although she had planned to get up early, she slept in and woke up when the sun was streaming through her bedroom window. She leapt out of bed, and hurried up the stream path to arrive in time to wave good-bye to Vanda. The horses were pleased to see her. Nat stamped his hoof just once, indicating impatience in a most gentleman-like manner. She tipped their feeds in and carefully scrutinised Treacle, to see if she was any fatter, but it was hard to tell.

After rummaging through the tack room, she had collected the things she needed and took them out into the yard to clean. As well as the saddle and bridle she had found an old pair of leather jodhpur boots in the far corner of the tack room, covered in filth and with a whole family of spiders nesting in the left hand one. She cleaned and polished them up and tentatively tried them on, they were a little big but would certainly be better than nothing. Then she tried a faded velvet riding cap, very old-fashioned and certainly would not pass any legal safety regulations these days but again – better than nothing. Dressed up like this she looked like a child out of an old-fashioned pony book where the impossible pony is secretly schooled to perfection and then wins the jumping class in the local gymkhana. In the pony books children often secretly rode ponies that didn't belong to them, and then everything turned out happily.

She was putting off the moment when she saddled up Treacle and mounted. Justifying the plan to herself. Perhaps she would win the special trophy in the jumping competition on the Sunday morning of the pony club camp. But it had all been arranged that she ride Beau and in that way, he could easily be the best jumper, but not with her riding. She had never even jumped.

Then her thoughts went full circle, if her riding was to improve before the camp then she had to practise, so that left Treacle. She went into the barn and led her out and tied her up. Then she groomed her, running the softest leather back body brush over her coat. Then she put the saddle on, taking ages deciding exactly how far behind the wither it should rest. She had to stop dilly-dallying. With renewed determination, she put the bridle on and adjusted it so that the bit was in the right position, with just one and a half wrinkles in the corner of the lips. Somehow this ride was going to be one of the defining moments of her life.

There was nothing more to do than mount. But still she dithered, perhaps she should lead Treacle down to the schooling field and ride her there. In the end, she decided that the yard was best, at least Nat was there, watching them through the open barn door.

She gathered up the reins and holding them with a large handful of mane, put her foot in the stirrup, and swung up into the saddle. She sat softly, making sure not to thump down on the mare's back. Treacle stood there quietly. Jenny looked down at her long, rather thin neck and watched her ears which were pricked forward. She was much more narrow and taller than the solid little Berry. It felt very precarious sitting in the saddle. They stood motionless for a minute then Jenny squeezed with her legs and they walked around the yard twice.

Then Jenny decided that nothing dramatic was going to happen. She would see if they could do a halt. Gently she fixed her hand and tried to stiffen her hips and Treacle stopped. Again, she gave the aid to walk forward and the mare walked on, then the aid to halt and she stopped. She seemed to have a soft mouth, and she was responsive to the lightest leg aid, but this was an enclosed place - it might be totally different in the big field. She squeezed with her legs to walk forward again and this time tried to turn her inwards to the left, feeling the inside rein and nudging her leg behind the girth on the outside. Then as she bent inwards, she reversed the aids and with gentle pressure on

118

the right rein and her left leg behind the girth Treacle turned obediently in an S-shape.

Jenny decided that they had gotten this far, they might as well go down to the training field. She slid off and spent a few minutes patting the little mare and talking to her softly, telling her how wonderful she was. Then they walked down the lane and through the five-bar gate at the bottom of the field. Again, Jenny procrastinated and decided to lead her once around the perimeter of the field. Then there was nothing else to do except ride.

She re-mounted and they walked quietly for the first ten minutes. Then Jenny knew that she had to do it. She took a firmer hold on the reins and squeezed her legs and they trotted. The mare's stride was longer than Berry's and much springier, and she seemed to be racing a little. Jenny felt herself unbalanced and as she slipped in the saddle Treacle tossed her head and sprang into a canter. Jenny desperately grabbed the pommel of the saddle and held on. The canter was lovely, more rocking and comfortable than Berry's, but very, very fast, almost a gallop. Jenny just clung on and tried not to lean forward, which would only encourage Treacle to go faster. Eventually, the little mare slowed down and Jenny manage to pull the left rein tighter so they went into a small circle. She had lost both her stirrups and when Treacle eventually trotted she just fell off, softly, plop into the green grass.

She sat there laughing, which was rather strange. It was the first time she had ever fallen off, and she was glad that it had been with Treacle. The little mare came to a stop and stood there staring at Jenny who was laughing, almost hysterically. The pony walked over and put her head down, sniffing her, as if to apologise.

"Oh Treacle, that was the first time I've ever fallen off, and it didn't hurt at all, I think we should try again, that was such fun!"

She mounted again and for some strange reason she felt filled with confidence. She just knew that Treacle was the one! They walked for at least twenty minutes and then she pushed her into a trot but this time in a small circle so she had more control and they didn't go so fast. Then taking a deep breath and holding onto the pommel of the saddle with one hand she sent her cantering down the long side of the field. This time she was more prepared and pulled upwards with her hand to bring her seat down securely into the saddle and kept her shoulders back so she wouldn't make the mistake of leaning forward. The canter felt glorious, better than anything she had ever imagined. Then she thought that probably she had been asking too much of Treacle who was still so poor. She managed to pull on the reins and they came to an awkward sliding stop. She jumped off and patted Treacle's neck for ages, then quietly led her up to the yard. She unsaddled her and hosed her down so there wasn't a sign that she had been ridden, then after giving her a handful of crushed barley she led her up to the field.

Nat was getting impatient in the stable thinking that he had been forgotten. Now that Jenny had her confidence she wondered if she might just lunge him. He did need exercise as it was going to be at least a week before Sofia came back and Vanda was too busy to ride. So, she dug out the lunge rein and whip and the cavesson headcollar and led him down to the field. She had read about it in her book and she knew that she had to stand in the centre of the circle, at the apex of an imaginary triangle with the lunge rein down one long side, and the whip down the other.

Luckily, Nat had been lunged endlessly before he was broken in and he was very obliging and went around her in a circle despite her inept commands and flapping whip. After a while she told him to canter and he did that as well. Then she halted him and set him off the other way and again he went well.

Jenny felt so pleased with herself. She believed that she really was going to develop into a young horsewoman. She was living the dream. She let Nat go in the field and he went and rolled in the dusty patch and wandered off to join Treacle who had her head down grazing.

"Now to work," she said to herself. She was determined to finish all the tack today but first she mucked out the stables. She carefully scraped up all the soiled sawdust and wheelbarrowed it down to the compost heap near the vegetable garden. Then she scraped the rest of the sawdust to the sides of the stables so that the ground would dry.

She returned to the tack room and began to clean each saddle until it shone and there was no speck of dirt or grime. When they were all cleaned there was still a tangled pile of bridles but Jenny was starving. She went into the scullery and scrubbed her hands then sat at the kitchen table and ate the sandwiches that Vanda had left her. If only life was like this every day, riding, training, and looking after horses, that was her idea of heaven. She had at least a week, and probably more and she was determined to make the most of it. She didn't want to ride Nat that would have been completely wrong but she thought it must be all right to lunge him to keep him fit. She would have to confess to Sofia that she had ridden Treacle but in her mind, it would all come right and Sofia would congratulate her and tell her that Treacle was to be hers.

The next week flew by for Jenny, every day was filled with activity and she felt that she was progressing marvelously. She made sure not to ride Treacle for more than thirty minutes as she was still so thin but after three days, she could canter a twenty-metre circle on either leg and she had even tried trotting over poles on the ground. She loved Treacle so much, she was so lovely and light, lively and fun to ride, moving like an elegant princess and they were developing a deep bond of friendship. Nat happily got lunged every day and she had managed to learn how to crack the lunge whip.

Vanda had praised her work in the tack room and she had agonised endlessly over how many saddles she might ask to have for herself. She didn't want to be greedy but it didn't seem that Vanda would really need them. If she could sell some of them then she could add substantially to her savings to buy herself a pony.

"Look what if you advertise them on eBay, I'm quite happy for you to keep the money, you deserve it after all this hard work. There is still another barn over there that I haven't been into, if you clean that out and find anything you could sell that as well," Vanda said to her after twelve days.

"Oh Vanda, that is so wonderful, thank you so much. You know I'm saving up for a pony," Jenny confided.

"That doesn't surprise me," said Vanda, who was very aware of Jenny's hopes and dreams, they were written all over the young girl's face.

"Sofia is coming back tomorrow you know," said Vanda.

"Yes, and then on Friday afternoon the camp is starting," said Jenny.

"You are going to be riding Beau aren't you?" said Vanda.

"Yes, that's right. Sofia has arranged it, she is very kind."

"I'll ring Allegra and see if she can come over on Friday morning and then she can give you a lesson so you start to get used to him. You know he is quite an amazing pony."

"Yes, I know when Izzie used to ride him in the shows, she would always win the turnout, the pony hack class and the jumping. He was quite famous as the best pony in the district."

That night Jenny walked slowly down the stream path. There was so much happening, good and bad, hope and disappointment swinging wildly through her heart. She tried to sort out her feelings. On the plus side, she was to get the money from selling the saddles and there might be amazing treasure in the old barn. She would start on that tomorrow. And she was going to ride Beau at the pony club camp which was the most amazing chance, and she knew that her riding was improving hugely, she felt much more confident, although she still had to jump at least she could canter properly without hanging onto the saddle. On the down side, Sofia was coming back so Treacle might be leaving within a week and she would never see her again, and Beau would go back to Penmar Hall and she would have nothing else to ride, and the summer holidays were almost over.

It was all too much she felt as if her head was bursting. She started to run, racing the stream that was burbling lazily beside her, she had to just ride the wave, and see where she washed up. At least there were possibilities but nothing was ever for certain. If only her parents could buy her a pony the way that Essie was bought ponies, one was no good so she got another. She shook her head and stamped her foot, pretending she was a wild pony, then she began to prance, like a high-stepping circus horse. She had to keep moving or she would burst. You only have the moment, she remembered her gran saying, and tomorrow was treasure seeking in the old barn, and the next day riding Beau. And perhaps Sofia would come back and tell her that Treacle was to be hers. Anything, or nothing, was possible!

Chapter Eighteen

On Thursday morning the weather was soft, cool, and misty, the hot endless summer days were dissolving and there was a chance of rain over the weekend, which would entirely ruin the pony club camp. Jenny lay in bed feeling sleepy, she had spent last night thinking too much. She had plenty to do emptying out the barn today, and also doing the horses, as Sofia probably wouldn't get back til mid-afternoon. But still she lay in bed wishing that she had magical powers and could chant a spell and everything would come right.

She heard Amanda shouting up to her, "Jenny! Jenny! It's that Zane, he's come for you."

She looked out the window and saw Zane was riding Blue, prancing and twirling, churning up the fine gravel on the stream path.

"Hey, Jen!" he called and waved.

"What is it Zane? Has something happened?" It was unusual for him to come to her house, it must be important.

"Yeah" he was almost shouting now. Jenny had never seen him so excited. "We're gonna live up at Treloar, with the 'orses, in the field. Vanda's goin' away and leavin' me Dad in charge. It was all arranged last night, it's gonna be great!"

"Wow!" shrilled back Jenny. She ran outside and down the garden, startling Blue into another frenzied twirling dance.

"Sorry," she called, slowing down, and speaking in a softer voice. "So, when are you moving?"

"Right now, I'm on my way up. C'm on, Dad's goin' by the road with the caravan and Ghost, and Himself trottin' along behind. We're to go and camp up in the big field, looking down over the stream."

"Wow! I can't believe it, that's so great for you. Hang on a minute and I'll come up with you!" Jenny dashed back inside to get dressed. She felt as if the world was tilting and twirling, like Blue, and maybe in all the change there would be a chance somehow for her and Treacle.

"I don't think Blue would take you up behind me," said Zane doubtfully.

"Definitely not," said Jenny emphatically, she had observed Blue enough to know that the last thing she wanted to do was piggy back on the skittery grey mare. "I'll just run up ahead of you, so as not to spook her."

She scampered up the path and Zane rode behind her. They got to the bottom gate and went up into the Treloar farm yard. Zane dismounted and they led the mare out onto the road so they could see Ghost carefully and steadily pulling the Gypsy caravan up the road. The brown horse, Himself, was tied on behind, walking briskly, looking around curiously. They pulled up at the top of the hill field and Vanda was there opening the gate for them. Blue, Zane, and Jenny walked down to join them.

"I think this would be a good place," said Vanda, leading the way down the field to a clump of small trees that were permanently bent like old women in the teeth of the wind. "It's not too far down to the stream for water and there's some shelter beneath the trees."

"All right," said Dane.

"Here you hold Blue, and I'll untie Himself," said Zane handing the reins over to Jenny. His father backed up the big Gypsy cob so that the caravan was sitting on even ground. They unhitched Ghost and led him out of the shafts. Vanda watched smiling, she felt all warm inside, almost as if her family had come home. She knew this was illogical. Dane was here because he had nowhere else to go. It was a practical solution to his problem. The police had begun to harass him, pointing out that he was not legally allowed to camp on the headland. So, she had offered for him to come and camp in the far field at Treloar. She had shaped the proposal as if he was doing her a favour, keeping an eye on the place while she was away. He had his pride and she was careful about this. She almost wished that she could somehow cancel her trip to Russia, so that she could be near him, but she knew that would be a fatal error. Softly, softly catchee monkey, as her mother used to tell her.

"Come up to the house, just this once, I've got some beer and I've made sandwiches," she said, indulging her instincts to mother him and Zane. Then thinking beer at this time in the morning was ridiculous, she wasn't thinking straight. Sofia was due back today and then the camp. The place was going to be buzzing.

"Okay," said Dane, agreeing to lunch down at the house. He didn't want to appear churlish. In exchange for a place to camp he was determined to earn his keep. Once Vanda had gone away, he would work at the farm house, cleaning out gutters, minor woodwork repairs, and some painting.

They let the horses go in the field. It was the first time they had been free to graze untethered but Dane had no qualms, he was sure they would co-exist peacefully. Blue set off up the hill, her long striding trot with her tail stuck out like a banner, she patrolled up and down the stone wall, neighing up to the moor.

"I 'ope she's not going to jump that wall," said Zane worried.

"She'll settle," said his father.

"She looks beautiful," said Jenny.

Ghost had wandered off down to the best patch of grass, his instinct was always to eat. Himself was a different horse since he had been gelded. He was much quieter and calmer, not exactly subdued, but tractable. He followed Ghost at a respectful distance and began to crop the nourishing Cornish grass.

Vanda led the way along the narrow track that skirted around the edge of the field. Dane followed her, his long legs striding out, his battered hat pulled down over his eyes, making him appear inscrutable. Jenny and Zane brought up the rear, chattering away.

The soft swirling rain had cleared and the sun struggled through dove grey clouds. Vanda felt an insane desire to make plans. She and Dane could ride together up on the moors. Perhaps even Zane could stay

126

and go to school with Jenny. They could run a family business, pony trekking across the moors. She even wondered what it would be like to have a beautiful, dark-skinned Gypsy baby girl, perhaps called Luna, born on a full moon. Oh God, she was going mad! If Dane even got a hint of her thoughts he would be away with the wind and she would never see him again. She felt like some stupid girl that read magazines at the hairdressers. This was just not going to happen. She nailed down her ridiculous dreams and concentrated on saying something non-threatening and vaguely intelligent.

When they got back to the yard Jenny asked where she would let Nat and Treacle out, she didn't think that they should go in the same field as Ghost.

"I think they can go in the lower field today, then they can see the other horses on the hill and get used to them being there," replied Vanda.

Dane and Vanda went inside for a while, but then he came out and said that he would sort out his camp, build a fireplace, and unpack the caravan. He was feeling a little overwhelmed and wanted some time alone. Vanda didn't offer to help. She was going shopping for supplies for the pony clubbers, there was lots for her to do.

She got back from the village and saw that the children had piled all sorts of junk in the yard. She realised then how awkward it was going to be.

"Jenny, I think we might need to change the plan. It's great that you've done all this, but I'm just wondering, it's not a good time to clutter things up with so many people arriving soon. Have you discovered anything amazing?"

"No, I don't think so," said Jenny, trying to hide the disappointment in her voice.

"Look anything that is obviously rubbish you can put in the back of the truck and I'll take it to the tip later this afternoon, otherwise just pile it neatly back in the shed, we can sort it out next week."

Then Dane appeared in the yard.

"I thought we might go for a ride up on the cliffs, I really need to give Himself some work, I think it's better if Zane rides him at the camp and not Blue, she's getting big now and it wouldn't be good for her."

"That sounds fun, I could come with you on Nat?" said Vanda.

Dane nodded brusquely and turned on his heel.

"All right Jenny would you mind bringing in Nat and saddling him up for me," said Vanda, "I have to go in and change."

Jenny went down to the field to catch Nat, leading him up to the yard to saddle him. She felt much more confident now when she was handling the horses. Then Vanda mounted and rode up the road. Dane was sitting on Himself at the gate, waiting for her.

Zane and Jenny started to pile stuff into the truck. The more they threw away the easier it would be to find something valuable. There were old scraps of timber and corrugated iron.

"Do you think any of these are good for anything?" Jenny asked Zane doubtfully, pointing at some of the rubbish.

"I don't think so the timber is low quality and rotting, and I don't think Vanda is planning on building a piggery or anything like that, which would need iron roofing."

They had almost finished clearing the yard when Sofia drove in with the empty horse trailer hooked up behind her four-wheel drive. She leapt out and shouted hello at the top of her voice. Jenny and Zane emerged from the barn, filthy, their hair sticking out on end.

"Goodness you two look a sight, what are you doing, cleaning up?" asked Sofia.

"How is Rimmi?" asked Jenny, hopping from one foot to another.

"Oh, he is better, it was teeth growing under his gum, he got operated on and now he is perfectly fine and he rides like a dream," said Sofia.

"Oh, I'm so pleased for you!" said Jenny.

"So where is Nat?" asked Sofia.

"Well Vanda took him for a ride with Dane," said Jenny wondering if this would be all right with Sofia.

"With Dane? Oh, that's right, that's her Gypsy friend. And I remember you Zane, you were riding that flighty pretty little grey mare."

Zane looked at her, not quite knowing what to say, he felt intimidated by her posh accent, she didn't sound friendly like Vanda.

Nothing was said about Treacle at all. Jenny tried to work out if this was a good thing, or a bad thing. If Sofia didn't even think to ask then it meant she didn't care about her at all. If Jenny piped up and told her how good the little mare was to ride then Sofia might automatically decide to sell her. It was a tricky situation.

"Come on let's finish off this barn," she said to Zane. Sofia carried her bag into the house.

It was a couple of hours before Vanda and Dane came back. Nat looked like he had had a good workout.

"Oh Vanda, you're back! It's great you've ridden Nat he probably needed it after more than a week off," said Sofia coming out in the yard to talk to her cousin.

"Allegra is bringing over Beau tomorrow morning so that Jenny can have a ride on him," said Vanda.

"Good-oh," said Sofia, but it sounded like she didn't really care.

"I'm going to bring Treacle up and put her in the stable," said Jenny.

"Look there's no need for that, she can stay down in the field," said Sofia. "There's going to be a lot to do tomorrow without cleaning out an extra stable. That reminds me Jenny I brought back a present. Here you are. It's one that I used to wear before I grew out of it." She handed over a riding helmet. "I never fell off on it so it should be fine."

129

"Oh, thank you so much," said Jenny, "it's brill, absolutely great."

"Well I suppose you'd better be off home, you're coming up tomorrow to ride Beau, yes?"

Jenny was thrilled at the riding helmet but she felt like she'd been kicked in the stomach, the way that Sofia dismissed her and virtually told her to go home.

"Now, Vanda, what is this about Dane living in the field," said Sofia, mischievously, her eyes sparkling. "Is he your boyfriend now?"

Vanda looked at Zane in embarrassment.

"Only you would say that," she said to Sofia crossly, and took Nat into the stable. Then she went back inside the house.

Zane decided at this point to go back to the camp. He didn't want to think about his Dad and Vanda together. Although he had occasionally wondered whether his father would find another woman. His mother always had new guys around, but no sooner did one appear than another would take his place. Zane hated it and just tried to be polite and disappeared into his bedroom. Some of them tried to be his friend, others were very casual and brushed him away. He hated to think of his mother with any of them.

*****

The next morning Jenny was up at Treloar early. She fed Nat, then caught Treacle and led her up to the small field next to the yard, with the shelter. She gave her an extra big feed. The little mare was looking good, she had put on weight, the poverty lines that ran down the side of her haunches seemed less pronounced. Then Jenny went back up and led Nat out and tied him up in the yard and mucked out his stable. She was determined to be as useful as possible and she knew that Sofia wasn't keen on stable work. She could see Vanda busy in the kitchen.

Before Sofia even surfaced, Allegra and Tristan arrived with Beau in the trailer. They led him down the ramp and Jenny watched. She couldn't believe that she was to ride this pony for the next three days.

130

He was beautifully groomed, perhaps a little too fat but he looked so smart in his dark blue rug with matching traveling bandages on his legs. His tail was wonderfully thick and perfectly smoothed.

"Izzie cleaned him up yesterday, and she even rode him round the park, just to get him back into the swing of things. I think he will go beautifully for you," said Allegra.

"Come on. Here's his tack, you can ride him first up and then we'll turn him out for the day."

"Gosh there are new horses up on the hill," said Allegra.

"Yes, they're Dane's horses, he's camping up there. Can you see his Gypsy caravan?"

"Oh yes! How pretty it looks! Like something out of a story book," said Allegra.

Jenny smiled to see how different Allegra was to Sofia. She seemed as soft and kind as butter, compared to Sofia's more robust and sarcastic approach to life.

Jenny rode Beau around the perimeter of the training field.

"You have a wonderful natural seat, and good posture. Now I want you to relax, stretch your legs down, lift the top of your head up towards the sky. That's good," said Allegra encouragingly.

They trotted and Jenny found the little chestnut gelding very easy to ride. He wasn't quite as springy as Treacle. He was more business-like, as if he knew how good he was, brimming over with self-esteem.

"I think we'll try some exercises," said Allegra. "Just keep trotting and I'm going up to get the lunge rein."

Jenny even tried a sitting trot as she had been reading about that in her book, but she found it very hard, she kept bouncing and went back to rising trot, keeping her hands as still as possible. She was a little mystified as to why they might need a lunge rein.

It all became clear when Allegra attached the rein to a headcollar that she buckled over the bridle. Jenny found herself trotting around in a smaller circle on the end of the lunge rein with her stirrups crossed in front of her and the reins knotted.

"Now hold onto the pommel and try pulling yourself down. That's brilliant see how smooth he is. Now I want you to try rising to the trot without stirrups."

Jenny tried her hardest but it was difficult, she felt the muscles in her legs aching.

"Now I'm going to get him to canter. I want you to hold on with your outside hand but I want you to raise your inside arm level with your shoulder and point to the centre of the circle."

Jenny thought it was strange but somehow it did seem to be helping her to really feel like she was part of the pony.

"Have you tried jumping at all?" asked Allegra.

"No," puffed Jenny, feeling her face getting redder and redder with exertion.

"Well I guess we've got this morning to get you jumping. Whoa! Halt! There isn't he good? He obeys spoken commands, so remember that. If all else fails talk to him. Now take your stirrups back but pull them up two holes shorter as you're going to be adopting a slightly different seat when you jump. You will need shorter stirrup leathers, but don't lean forward until the horse leaves the ground to go over the jump then you swing back to the upright position as the horse lands. We'll keep him on the lunge and I'll just position a small jump on one side, and then another on the other side of the circle. Are you up for it?"

"Oh yes!" said Jenny, finally she was going to jump and only just in time for the camp.

She sat still on Beau and got her breath back while Allegra dragged over a couple of poles and arranged them on top of some small plastic supports.

"It's only small, perhaps 30 centimetres, it will be nothing for such a clever well-trained pony like Beau. You just have to sit there and get used to the feeling."

Jenny's heart was racing, a mixture of excitement and the thrill of fear. She had waited so long for this opportunity.

"We won't get him to trot over them, it's probably easier if he canters, then it will just be a large canter hop."

Beau, perfectly trained, cantered from the walk on the verbal command and Jenny sat there. She remembered to sit upright and kept her gaze between his ears. She was amazed at how it felt, so easy, so longed for and then it was like a great big exciting canter, not exactly flying but she could imagine what it would be like with a bigger jump. They went around the circle another half dozen times, then round the other way.

"You're doing very well!" said Allegra. "Now we'll take you off the lunge and let's see if you can canter him over the jump on your own. I'll rearrange them in a line, perhaps five canter strides apart. So, you go to the bottom of the field and canter up, then jump, five more strides and jump again. You just sit still and keep him straight, he'll do the rest."

Jenny was filled with elation. This was going to be proper jumping. She trotted to the bottom of the field and turned the corner and pushed him into a canter. She sat still and carefully kept contact on her reins. She could feel him see the jump, adjust his stride, and take off perfectly, then she counted, "one, two, three, four and five", and they were over the second jump.

"Keep him cantering around the corner down the long side and do it three times more, then I think that will be enough excitement for one day," called out Allegra.

This time was even better Jenny felt as if she was more in control. She knew that Beau was so well-trained that anyone could sit on him and point him at the jumps but she felt that finally she was on her way to being a good rider. She wished she could go on practising for hours.

133

"I'll take him up and hose him down," she said when they had negotiated the line of jumps four times. "Do you know if he is going in the field, or the stable?"

"I'll check with Sofia, I'm not sure how many stables are going to be available," said Allegra.

Jenny was filled with hope - everything was going to come right.

"How many have we got to be stabled. Treacle can stay in the small paddock by herself, we don't want her chased by any of the other horses. There's Nat who has to come in at night, and Del, and Beau who are all stabled, but I think the rest of the ponies can go in the middle field. There's three extra stables in case we need them." Sofia was taking charge now.

"Should Beau go out for the rest of the day?" asked Sofia.

"Yes, put him out today and then he can come in tonight," said Allegra. "I'm bringing Skydancer over tomorrow but I'll take her back after she's been ridden. You know that Izzie will muck out for Del."

"So that's good, there's plenty of sawdust in that small shed," said Sofia. "The Tregonnings are going to be here mid-afternoon to start setting up the tents, so let's go in and have a coffee and go through our lists to make sure everything is ready."

Jenny led Beau down to the field. She patted him before she let him go. He was such a smart pony, but quite self-possessed, as if he didn't depend on anyone. Treacle was different, she needed love. Jenny didn't go in to lunch she stayed outside petting Treacle, this might be the last chance she had of being alone with her. There would be no time during the camp and then Sofia was leaving, presumably taking her back to Hampshire.

Chapter Nineteen

"Just do as you're told," snapped Nick Tregonning impatiently, addressing his younger brother Dom, who would do anything to get out of hard work. It was all very well claiming to be artistic but he had to pull his weight like everyone else.

"It's all a bit regimental," said Dom in an affected accent.

"Sometimes I think you think you're living in a novel," said Nick loftily. He had heard that expression on one of the DVDs that his mother watched and had decided that it fitted Dom to a 'tee'.

"That here, that there," grumbled Tom, the youngest Tregonning at just twelve years old, who felt constantly squashed down by his much bigger brothers. He hated being the youngest, and his father expected him to work just as hard as the other two. He had a little pony mare, only 12.1 hh, named Goldie. Secretly he'd been practising and the other day they had cleared a substantial jump at four feet. He was the most ambitious of the three brothers and he was determined to be a professional rider when he grew up. Dairy farming was not for him!

The camping area was almost ready for the influx of young riders and their ponies on the eve of Goonhilly Pony Club camp. All the tents were erected. A big camp fire had been constructed out of smooth stones that had been fetched up from the stream bed, and a nest of twigs, leaves and wood was arranged ready to be lit. A temporary hitching rail had been set up. The Tregonnings' ponies were already tied up there. Although Nick's horse was not a pony, he was a solid plain cob well over 15 hh. Then there was Dom's flashy dark grey mare, Guinevere, and Goldie.

Vanda was in the kitchen of the farm house checking through a list to make sure she had all her supplies to produce seven meals for five adults, and nine children. She had a large pot of beef stew simmering on the gas stove, twenty-six large potatoes wrapped in foil in the larder ready to be baked later in the coals of the fireplace, two large tins of home-baked cookies, three layered iced cakes, four crates of soft drinks, a dozen cartons of orange juice and that was just for starters. She had been planning her menus for the last week, she liked to be organised.

Time seemed to be rushing along now. Her departure date to go to Russia was mid-September, just three weeks away. With Dane living up on the hill she felt that there was a chance that their friendship might develop into a relationship. But she couldn't put off her plans just in that vain hope. That didn't fit her idea of herself at all. She refused to be one of those women whose life was defined by her relationship with a man. She also had to face the fact that she and Dane were probably nothing more than a figment of her hopeful imagination. She vowed to herself that if nothing definitive happened between them this weekend then she would go to Russia. Perhaps when she came back Dane would have realised what she meant to him. At least she had pinned him down to staying here while she was away, he was to look after the place, so he couldn't just go off, disappearing in a wisp of smoke like a changeling. Then it occurred to her that now he was more settled she might come back and find that he had installed a girlfriend. On her property! She shook her head in annoyance, she had to stop thinking like this.

Jenny and Zane were busy organising the haynets and water buckets for the ponies who were to be tied to the hitching rail. Earlier they had put down beds of sawdust in extra stables. Xanthe's mother had rung Vanda at the last moment and literally demanded that Xanthe's dressage horse, Gemstone, should be stabled. She had insisted that she couldn't be let out in a field with a herd of common ponies. Vanda felt intense dislike for this woman and her ghastly daughter.

After the annoying call from Xanthe's mother the phone rang again. This time it was good news. Mrs Bowles was ringing to say that she couldn't come to the camp, she had been called away urgently. Her sister was in hospital. Vanda assured her that they would be perfectly capable of running the event without her.

Maddie Cross's parents did not have a fancy horse box like Xanthe's, nor did they have a cattle truck like the Tregonnings, not even a horse trailer pulled by the family sedan. When she was able to get to shows, Maddie went in Ned's old truck that was a type of local bus, carrying local riders and ponies around to events. Maddie only lived ten miles from Treloar so she decided to ride, her mother had agreed to take her gear over in the car. She set out early and rode slowly, just walking and trotting very slowly along the twisting narrow coast road. Xanthe's horse box had passed her, not bothering to slow down and forced them into a hedge.

"Isn't that Madeline Cross?" asked Xanthe's mother.

"Yes, on that awful brown creature. Really, I'd be embarrassed to be seen riding such an ugly horse. I suppose it matches her carrot hair," laughed Xanthe unkindly.

Xanthe's mother smiled indulgently. She was not the sort of adult who reproved her child when she made uncharitable remarks. In fact, she was proud of the fact that Xanthe had developed such a superior attitude, it showed that they had class. They drove into the outskirts of St Bliz to pick up Essie.

"Do we really have to keep helping this girl?" asked Xanthe. "Now that they've paid for Boxer, I thought we could give it a miss."

"I know darling but I do rather like her mother. I believe that the father, who lives somewhere near London is rather important in the city. It always pays to know the right people."

"Well look at the cottage!" exclaimed Xanthe as they came to a smooth halt outside the little stone house.

"Yes, but the parents are separated and apparently there is yet to be a financial settlement. I wouldn't be surprised if Belinda didn't buy something more upmarket later. You know your father still has several more of those houses in the new development to sell, we were thinking that she might buy one of them."

Xanthe's father was a land developer and he always encouraged his wife to be friends with potential buyers.

Vanda could hear a vehicle coming up the hill and she went out to wave them into the yard. Really it was Sofia who should be doing this. Xanthe's mother stopped the rather flashy silver horse truck in the road outside the house. She climbed out and smoothed down her elegant outfit.

"I say, could you unload these horses please," she called out to Vanda when she saw her approaching, as if she was the hired help.

"I think the girls should be able to unload their own ponies," said Vanda disagreeably. "You can't park there for long as you're blocking the road. You need to unload and carry everything down through the yard to the field below by the stream where the children will be camping." Then she turned around and walked off leaving Xanthe's mother looking annoyed at the very obvious put down.

"Well really!" she exclaimed. "I expected better treatment than that."

Xanthe was lowering the back ramp and Essie was moving from one foot to the other, looking embarrassed.

She rushed up the ramp and untied Boxer and then tried to pull the pin out of the divider so she could lead him down.

"Here let me do that," said Xanthe impatiently. Her mother was not going to carry luggage down to the field, instead she went down and called out to Nick Tregonning.

"I say! You! Can you come up here and carry down the equipment!"

Nick looked up and calling to Dom to come and help strode up the hill. He took charge of unloading, wondering just how much equipment two girls and two horses were going to need.

Essie led Boxer down, also carrying her heaviest bag. Xanthe was holding her dressage horse, a tall elegant pale palomino mare.

"She is to go in a stable, you couldn't possibly expect her to go down there with the ponies. It's all been arranged," she said haughtily.

"Yes, Vanda told me," said Nick, refusing to take offence. "The stable is ready for her in that barn, the loose box closest to the door. You do realise that you will be responsible for mucking out, don't you?"

138

Xanthe looked at him and smiled.

"I rather thought you might do that for me Nick," she said in silky tones.

Dom was laughing, his merry little eyes alight.

"Oh Nick, obviously she's your girlfriend!"

"Don't be so ridiculous," said Nick, not quite knowing how to react. "Pick up those sacks and put them in the tack room."

Sometime later, Maddie arrived. She'd carefully wound exercise bandages around her mare's legs, hoping that she wasn't going to suffer too much damaging concussion from such a long ride along the road. She dismounted in the farm yard and stood there uncertainly, not sure what to do. Vanda saw her from the kitchen window and came out to meet her.

"Oh hello, my name's Maddie Cross, I'm here for the pony club camp," she said politely.

"Oh well, I'm Vanda, glad to meet you, go down through the gate and you'll see the others camping in the field."

"Oh yes of course, I'm sorry to bother you," said Maddie. Her shiny bright carrot red hair made her look like she had a halo in the late afternoon light.

Vanda was finding this invasion of young people into her territory a little overwhelming. It was not what she was used to. She saw that Zane had joined the group down by the field and was making himself useful carrying up buckets of water from the stream and emptying them into an old trough that they had placed there for the weekend. Dane was nowhere in sight, no doubt hiding up in his camp. This was absolutely not his sort of thing.

So, everybody was there with their ponies; the three Tregonning brothers, Xanthe and Essie, Zane and Jenny, Izzie and Madeline. Sofia decided that she and Vanda should go down and make some sort of speech welcoming everyone and letting them know what they would be doing. Vanda wasn't keen.

"No, you go down Sofia, you make the speech, I'll just finish the dinner, then you can send some of the kids up to take it down, they can eat on the long trestle table that has been set up near the camp fire."

"Are you sure, in a way you're the hostess," said Sofia.

"No, really public speaking is just not my sort of thing," said Vanda, turning away to go back to the kitchen and prevent any further discussion of the subject.

Sofia strode down to the stream, and shouted for the children to gather around.

"Hello everyone," she began, "I'm Sofia and with my sister Allegra, we'll be doing most of the instruction. Vanda Peregrine who owns Treloar and has kindly let us all have the weekend here is doing the catering. I want to thank the three Tregonning boys for helping set up the camp. Jolly well done chaps!"

"First up the schedule is this, more or less, tomorrow we'll gather in that long field there and do some schooling. We're not sure yet whether we'll have one group or two. Then Allegra is to do a masterclass on her mare Skydancer, we'll choose the rider to do that tomorrow morning but by necessity it will probably be someone with quite long legs. Then tomorrow afternoon we'll do some jumping. If by chance it rains, and it doesn't look like it will, then we'll have to go inside and do some theory. I thought if some of you would like you could build a couple of cross-country jumps going into the stream across and up the bank. There's a suitable place just upstream and round the bend. Jumping water is probably one of the most difficult elements in the cross-country so it would be good experience."

"Well I'm certainly not going to risk Gemstone's legs jumping in and out of water and up the bank!" said Xanthe defiantly. Essie saw that she was meant to agree with her but on the other hand everyone else was staring at Xanthe distastefully.

"Well if you're not game and your horse isn't capable then don't" said Nick a little crossly. He had decided that he didn't much like Xanthe's attitude at all, he much preferred Maddie who seemed to be a very nice person. Sofia ignored the interruption.

"On Sunday morning, we're having a show jumping competition and my sister, Allegra has kindly donated a huge cup for the winner. Then after Sunday lunch I guess there will be gymkhana games. Now I would like each of you to introduce yourselves and your pony for the weekend then we can have supper."

Everyone clapped and cheered and Sofia breathed a sigh of relief. She suddenly felt like she'd slipped into the adult category, she was no longer a child, and it didn't feel that bad at all! She gestured for Nick to step up and introduce himself.

"Hello," he began, pushing his hair back nervously and clearing his throat, "I'm Nick and I've been a member of Goonhilly Pony Club ever since I could ride. I've got my horse here today, he's a very sensible cob and we call him Bob."

"Bob the cob!" shouted out Dom, never losing a chance to make fun of his older brother.

"All right Dom, you'd better come up and introduce yourself then," said Nick, thankfully going back to sit on the ground with the others.

Dom stepped forward. He had almost shoulder length hair which he considered 'arty' and he was very good looking. Jenny sighed as she looked at him, he was gorgeous she thought to herself, and apparently he was also a brilliant rider.

"I'm Dom, and I've got a very pretty mare Guinevere, and this is my younger brother, Tom,"

"Hi, I'm Tom and Goldie is my mare and she's the best jumper in the world," announced the youngest Tregonning.

"Jenny," said Sofia. "You're next."

"Hi, I'm Jenny Salmon and I live in St Bliz," then she paused, it was as if she was doing that thing where she was the 'girl from the village' again. "And Izzie has lent me her wonderful pony Beau to ride this weekend," she finished. She couldn't help looking sideways at Xanthe and Essie who both had their mouths open in surprise and annoyance. Neither of them had any idea that Jenny even knew Izzie Littleton!

"Essie!" called out Sofia, not missing the expression on Xanthe's face. She'd gathered from what Jenny had said that Xanthe was not a nice person and now it seemed the rumours were true. She would make certain that the little madam wasn't picked for the dressage masterclass.

"Hello, I'm Essie and I am riding my pony Boxer, who is a beaut pony, he used to belong to Xanthe."

"Xanthe," called out Sofia.

"Good afternoon," said the young woman haughtily tossing back her blond hair and pouting a little, her rosebud mouth had been carefully outlined with pink lip gloss. "I'm Xanthe and my mare, Gemstone, is an experienced dressage horse, she's a palomino and I'm in the process of teaching her to jump as well, but only show jumps I don't want her spoiled with any cross-country."

Jenny was interested in seeing Gemstone. She wasn't tied up to the hitching rail like all the others, she was up in a stable, apparently Xanthe's mother had insisted on that.

"Maddie," said Sofia.

"Hi, I'm Maddie Cross and I've been a member of Goonhilly Pony Club for years now. I'm so happy that things are happening again and I would like to thank Sofia, Allegra and Vanda for making it all possible." She smiled around in a friendly fashion

"Your horse?" queried Sofia.

"Yes, of course, my faithful steed is Cinnamon, well I call her Cinnie and she was a fantastic jumper but most of all my best friend."

Sofia made a mental note, Maddie was the obvious choice for the masterclass.

"Zane lives here at Treloar and he's riding a very promising young gelding called Himself." Sofia smiled at Zane who was looking painfully shy. "Apparently, he's very full of himself," she explained.

"Zane or the horse?" called out Dom, who fancied himself a wit.

"The horse of course," said Sofia smiling. "Oh, and not to forget Izzie," who stumbled up and stood in front of the group.

"Hello everyone, I'm Izzie Littleton," then she stopped, feeling embarrassed. My horse is Del and he's the best horse in the world, well I think so anyway."

"So that's it, nine riders and two days of fun and let's hope that we all learn lots this weekend, and get to be good friends, that's what pony club is all about!" said Sofia in her best imitation of a Pony Club Commissioner.

Everyone clapped then and Jenny jumped up with Zane and Izzie and they ran up to the farm house to collect the food. Sofia was marveling at her new self that seemed to be emerging unbidden, it was almost as if she was channelling Henrietta with her middle-class values and sense of 'doing the right thing'.

Dinner was wonderful, there was more than enough food and everyone ate until they were sated. They drifted back into small friendship groups. Quite surprisingly, Zane was talking earnestly and seriously to Izzie. Xanthe was holding court in front of Essie and the good-natured Maddie, who seemed to bear no-one any ill will.

Tom had attached himself to Jenny and was confiding in her, "I'm very keen to do more jumping," he explained. "My brothers think that I'm just a kid and Goldie is quite small, but I personally believe that she has a great future."

"Well I love her colour, Sofia has just bought a pony the same colour and type at Camborne Horse Sale," she said. "Perhaps they're related?"

143

"Well we don't know her breeding at all. We got her as an unbroken weanling from the horse sale as well and we've kind of grown up together. I broke her in myself," said Tom proudly.

Once the plates were put away Sofia pointed them to a pile of painted oil drums and poles and suggested they organise themselves into a work party and try and build a set of cross-country jumps across the stream.

"Don't forget to think about strides," she called out to them as most of them threw themselves into the project.

Chapter Twenty

The sun was shining straight through the thin surface of the tent wall when Jenny woke early on Saturday morning. It promised to be a glorious late summer day. She stumbled out trying not to wake the other girls. She went over to the boys' tent to rouse Zane.

"Come on!" she whispered. "Let's get the fire going and we can make everyone a cup of tea."

"All right," said Zane, coming out fully dressed as if he had slept in his clothes.

He raked over the coals from last night, and put some dry grass on top of the embers, then he knelt down and blew softly on it. A little flame curled around and he put some dry twigs on it and then some pieces of wood.

"You're awfully good at that," said Jenny admiringly.

"Well I've 'ad plenty of practice haven't I?" he said casually.

"Do you know if you're staying down here?" asked Jenny.

"No Mum won't agree, I'm to go back to London on Wednesday."

"Wednesday," echoed Jenny. Somehow, she had thought he wouldn't go away, now that he and Dane had moved to Treloar.

The other children began to emerge from their tents, drowsy and stretching and rubbing their eyes.

"Oh, jolly good show!" said Nick, in hearty tones, like a character out of an Enid Blyton novel. "Come on Dom let's go and catch the ponies. Come on you girls grab your halters it's time to give them their morning feed."

They straggled off and Jenny and Zane set out the mugs and filled them with warm milky tea with lots of sugar.

"Oh, this is fun!" exclaimed Maddie, sipping the hot sweet tea. She had been up earlier and had already fed Cinnie.

Eventually, the ponies were all caught and standing in a row tied to the hitching rail, each with a feed and a bucket of water. They looked content, in a bunch together, swishing their tails and waving their heads at each other in mock ferocity.

"So, this masterclass," said Nick addressing Jenny. "Do you know who is going to be chosen?"

Jenny shrugged, but secretly she felt pleased that she was recognised by the others as Sofia's special friend and confidante.

Sofia came down the path from the farm house carrying a large frying pan and a plate piled high with sliced bacon, and the tomato ketchup.

"I thought you might like to cook your own breakfast," she said.

"Bacon, I love bacon," said Nick, taking over responsibility for the cooking.

At nine o'clock everyone was mounted and under instructions from Nick, who was really getting into his stride and becoming positively bossy.

"I want you all riding around at the walk and trot to warm up," he had announced in an authoritative voice.

Allegra, dressed very smartly in bright white jodhpurs and a lemon and blue checked shirt, with a neat stock tied around her neck and fastened with a silver tie pin, came hurrying down the path.

"Right, now, everyone we're going to do a full tack inspection before we start. If you could just line up in order of height, please. I think that means you at the head of the line, Nick"

The pony club members shuffled back and forth disagreeing over whether it was the height of the rider, or the height of the horse and Xanthe claimed that Gemstone was at least two inches taller than Bob.

"He just looks big because he's as wide as a barrel," she declared scornfully.

Allegra and Sofia went down the line, checking the tack, particularly the stitching, especially where the leather and metal were attached, as that was the point where things came apart. Then finally everyone's equipment was declared safe and they were all riding around the field again.

"We're not having that ghastly Xanthe in the masterclass," said Sofia emphatically in a low voice.

"All right, it's got to be Maddie. She does seem to be a sweet girl and she's easily the best rider of the lot. Hasn't she been over riding at Max Winters?" replied Allegra.

"Yes, that's right, she's Max's golden girl at the moment. She would have been my choice," replied Sofia

"All right, I want you to tighten up your reins, half halt and transition to working trot," Allegra called to the riders.

"What's a half halt?" asked Jenny.

"Does anyone here know what a half-halt is?" Sofia asked. She had read somewhere that a good teacher should always throw the question back to the class.

"You push your horse in, compress like a spring, as if you're asking for a halt, then you relax the rein contact and he lowers his head and maintains increased impulsion with his hind legs," said Maddie, when no-one else seemed willing to contribute anything.

"Yes, that's good," said Allegra. "So, someone else, why do we half-halt? Xanthe?"

Xanthe opened her mouth and shut it again.

"Okay, Maddie, do you know why we use half-halts?"

"To signal to the horse that we are going to do a transition, or to ask for more collection, just generally to get their attention."

"Yes, that's good," said Allegra.

They all tried half-halts for twenty minutes and some of them got it, some didn't. Essie was having trouble just to keep up with Boxer, he seemed very heavy on her hands. In contrast, Jenny was finding it amazingly easy to do it on Beau, who had probably been half-halted most of his ridden life. When she got the timing right, she could feel him coming together then dropping his head into a better position. Xanthe was angry, of course she knew what a half-halt was, she did it all the time, but it was so natural, so incorporated into her riding style that she didn't think about it consciously. Nick didn't really see the point of telling the horse you were going to stop and then not stopping. Dom wasn't that bothered one way or the other, just slopped along with Guinevere's beautiful stride which always made him look like he was a better rider than he really was. Tom tried it with Goldie but couldn't quite get the letting the tension loose on the reins quickly enough, he had to really concentrate to let go just a second after he had given the halting aid. Zane tried and found that Himself seemed to go much better with a progressive aid. He would have to tell Dad about it, not that Dane would be much interested, he always curled up his long nostrils at this type of riding.

"All right, everyone!" called Allegra, wishing that she had some sort of thing to amplify her voice, she found it hard to shout out in the large meadow, with the sound of the stream burbling in the background.

"Now, I want you to dismount and go and tie your horses up to the hitching rail with their halters, make sure they all have water in their buckets, and then come back and I want Maddie to ride Skydancer, please."

Xanthe was furious, that Maddie had been chosen for the masterclass, over her! Her mother had assured her that she was going to be picked! She set her face in a sullen scowl and thought about complaining but she couldn't be bothered. They would soon see that Maddie was hopeless and wouldn't have a clue how to ride such a highly trained horse. And there was no way she was going to tie Gemstone on a hitching rail. She rode up to the farm yard slowly, she would untack and put the mare in the stable. She wasn't going to be lumped in with the common herd!

Maddie was genuinely thrilled to be picked, it was not at all what she had expected. She led Cinnie over to the makeshift hitching pole and buckled her headcollar on over the bridle.

"I'll always love you, no matter what," she said soothingly, in case Cinnie's feelings might be hurt that her mistress was going to ride the outstandingly beautiful Skydancer. Cinnie looked unfazed and thoughtfully took a mouthful of water, staring into the distance, thinking mysterious horse thoughts.

"I always wonder what you're thinking?" murmured Madeline.

"What did you say?" asked Jenny.

"Oh, I was just talking nonsense to Cinnie, don't worry about me," said Madeline, reddening a little, her complexion clashing unbecomingly with her frizzy carrot hair. "I better go over and get going." She hurried back to the big meadow and watched Allegra riding Skydancer around. She had never seen such a magnificent horse, the big silver mare seemed to float over the top of the ground with her long, extended trot strides, her toes pointed like a ballerina. This was going to be the most fantastic experience!

"Sofia can you just talk them through what I'm doing," Allegra called out.

Sofia got them all to stand at the far end of the field where the judge would have been positioned. She explained about the way in which dressage tests were marked.

"Each movement is out of ten. The judge begins with the mark of ten then deducts points for different faults, or that is how it is meant to happen." Then she went on to stress the issues that were particularly important.

"Straightness is the most important at this level, then flexion to each side. Most horses are naturally one-sided. One reason for this is that as foals in their mothers' wombs horses are curved around, often to

149

the left, sometimes to the right. This brings about a natural tendency to bend that way. There is something called the German scales of training which include six things, rhythm, looseness, contact and acceptance of the bit, impulsion, straightness and collection. You can see that Allegra is focusing on rhythm now which is the first step."

"What is looseness?" asked Nick, tending to pedantry. He liked to be clear on everything. In fact, he was a little sceptical about dressage. He didn't really understand it. Sofia wished that Allegra would explain, she knew there was a German word for it.

"It basically means an acceptance of the rider and letting itself be pushed through and at the same time also to be relaxed." She watched Allegra and Skydancer a little critically. They certainly looked good together, Allegra seemed to have improved her riding lately, which was odd, considering she was down here, missing out on her usual routine of endless, tedious hours of professional coaching. Sofia had to admit that Skydancer looked better than ever. They cantered and the mare wasn't leaning on the bit at all, she seemed to be achieving perfect 'self-carriage'.

"The horse should always be energised and showing good forward movement, but also being very calm. In the halts, you have to be straight and the horse standing square. Then immobility is important."

Allegra rode over to the group.

"Okay Maddie, you're up now, let's see how you go," she said. "I want you to do some twenty metre circles at the working trot and canter first then we'll try some more advanced moves."

Sofia stood back and watched Maddie on Skydancer. She was truly a natural rider, holding the reins like silk ribbons, carrying out every suggestion that Allegra made. Soon they were extended trotting across the diagonal and Skydancer look as if she was floating on air. Then they moved on to half-passes and finished with one beat tempi changes, where Skydancer looked like she was skipping, with a flying change every stride. They finished with a perfect square halt. And the

150

pony clubbers burst into spontaneous applause, except for Xanthe who stood there with her arms defensively folded in front of her.

"That was so well done!" said Allegra. Maddie dismounted and Allegra led Skydancer back up to the stable. The rest of the pony clubbers straggled over to the camping area where Vanda had set up trestle tables loaded with a huge variety of sandwiches on white and brown bread and plates of pumpkin scones.

"Oh, I am so hungry!" said Tom, his little eyes lit up at the sight of food. He always ate as much as he could, hoping that soon he would be as tall as Dom.

*****

After lunch Sofia went down to inspect the water cross-country jumps that the children had set up. They had put a line of four large, oil drums lying on their sides on the lip of the stream with about a two-foot drop into the water. The bed of the stream was sandy here, clear of stones so the horses wouldn't wrench their legs. It was about two strides across the water which was about two-feet deep, then up a bank one stride and then another line of drums. It was well done, and easy enough for all of them. The drums were kept in place by poles that were placed in front and behind them, so they wouldn't roll.

"You've done well here," said Sofia to Nick who had come with her.

"It should be fun. At least it's warm if any of us end up falling off into the stream."

"Yes, falling into the water at a public event in the middle of bitter winter is absolutely horrid!" said Sofia.

They went back to the camping ground where most of the children were sitting on the edge of the stream, their bare feet dangling in the cool water. Jenny and Zane were paddling, flinging water at Dom and Tom.

Sofia took her boots off and waded in with them, it was so hot, the sun beating down, the air thick with haze and insects humming. The tangerine heads of the Cornish lilies dipped and bowed towards the surface of the moving water. The sweet scent of the flowering heather flowed down from the moor and there was the faint twitter of tiny birds in the ferns lining the sides of the stream.

"So how are you liking Beau?" Sofia asked Jenny.

"Oh, he is marvelous, I think he must be the most brilliant pony in the world," said Jenny, who had been amazed at how easy it was when she was riding a perfectly trained pony. But she was feeling increasingly anxious about Treacle. In the end she hadn't told anyone, not even Zane, how she had been riding the little mare. There just hadn't been the right moment. Sofia never said anything about Treacle at all.

"Treacle has improved in condition in the last few weeks," Jenny said tentatively, screwing up her courage to make the confession.

"Is that that taffy pony up there?" asked Tom coming to join them in the middle of the stream.

"Shall we go up and look at her?" asked Jenny. She wanted to talk to Sofia away from the others and this seemed like the moment. There wasn't much time left, this might be her last chance.

"All right," said Sofia wading back to the bank of the stream, wiping her feet dry on the grass and putting her boots back on.

The three of them, Jenny, Tom, and Sofia walked up the hill. Jenny felt sick with hope and fright, so much depended on the next half hour. So much depended on what Sofia might say.

Treacle was standing in the depths of her field shelter built of thick granite stone. She had a pretty blue-edged day rug wrapped around her to keep the flies off. It also hid her ribs that were still just visible and her gaunt haunches. She nickered happily at the sight of Jenny, she loved her secret treats. Jenny gave her a handful of cut up and cored apple and unbuckled her rug and pulled it off. Her coat was much improved but not yet glossy with good health.

"She's pretty, and just like a bigger version of Goldie, perhaps they have the same breeding, they both did come through Camborne horse sale," said Tom. "What's she like to ride?"

Sofia said nothing and Jenny knew this was the perfect moment to speak up. To say, 'oh she is brilliant to ride, quite well-schooled'. She opened her mouth but no words came out.

"We have no idea, we've not done anything with her yet," said Sofia. "Would you like to try her out for us Tom?"

Jenny went into shock, totally horrified, all her dreams were turning into a horrible nightmare.

"I could ride her," burst out Jenny, unable to keep her anguish in check.

"Well, let Tom have first go then see how she goes," said Sofia carelessly. "Do you think you could find some tack for her?" she asked Jenny. Of course, Jenny could. She had it all prepared carefully cleaned after every riding session that she'd had on the mare in the preceding weeks. She walked up to the tack room and got it off the peg, her feet felt like lead, somehow, she knew this was not going to turn out well.

Treacle stood quietly while they saddled her and Tom ran back down to get his riding hat.

"Come on!" Sofia called. "Let's see what you're made of." She was having a flashback to when Rimmi had unceremoniously thrown her. She hoped Treacle wasn't going to be the same. Jenny knew that Treacle wouldn't buck, or rear, or bolt. She would behave perfectly and Tom was going to get all the credit.

Her predictions came true. In fact, Treacle seemed to go even better for Tom than she had for herself. They executed some perfect circles first at rising trot then a well-balanced rhythmic canter.

"Well this is good," said Sofia thoughtfully. Jenny looked at her, was she thinking how much she could sell Treacle for?

153

"She is absolutely brilliant!" said Tom. "Could I try her over one of the low jumps?"

"Well if you want to," said Sofia. The little pony jumped neatly, tucking her small black hoofs up and clearing it by several generous inches.

"All right we don't want to overdo it, especially not in this heat, and she's still a bit poor," said Sofia. Jenny looked down at the ground, it seemed as if she wouldn't get to ride at all.

"You know Dad has promised me a new pony, now that Goldie is a bit small. I love her, do you think we could buy her?"

Jenny stood there feeling the tears welling up in her eyes. This was worse than anything she had imagined. Well that wasn't entirely true, Sofia could have decided to send the pony back to the sale to be sold for meat.

"Could you tell me how much, if you were going to sell her?" asked Tom.

"Well if you could take her straightaway I would say £1500," said Sofia, thinking how neatly this was all going to work out. She had entirely forgotten about Treacle in all the drama of Rimmi's teeth, she would make more than £1000 profit. Perhaps there was a reward for virtue in volunteering for this camp.

"Dad might think that's a bit much, he's a bit of a one for a bargain," said Tom. "Seeing as you bought her at the sale."

Sofia looked at him shrewdly.

"Well since it's such a good home I might be a little bit negotiable," she said. "If he wants to buy her then he'd better come and look at her and then we can talk. Otherwise I take her back to Hampshire on Monday morning."

So as far as Jenny could see it was all settled. If Treacle didn't get sold to Tom then she would be taken away. She knew that Sofia had paid much less than £1500! She would certainly make a good profit.

She felt so sad. It was as if every hope she had was dashed, first Berry sold so quickly, Beau just for one blissful weekend, and now Treacle sold to Tom. Again, she would be left without a pony to ride.

She walked back down to the stream where the others were sitting, feeling utterly downcast. She tried to cheer herself up, to make the most of the weekend riding Beau but it was Treacle, she had loved, like a secret love affair that had all gone wrong. She didn't know which was worse Treacle going back to Hampshire never to be seen again, or watching Tom flying around jumping courses at future local shows.

Chapter Twenty-One

At two o'clock Sofia shouted to everyone to get saddled up. While the pony clubbers were riding their horses around to warm up, Vanda and Dane came down to the field to help with the jumps. Sofia gave them instructions and they built a course.

"Oh, look at that!" said Xanthe in a stage whisper to Essie. "It's that awful Gypsy that lives down at the headland." Zane flashed a hateful look at her.

"He's my father!" he hissed at her with such vehemence that for a moment Xanthe felt a little nervous.

Then Sofia shouted out instructions. They were all to jump the three jumps set at forty centimetres and then continue to the fifty-centimetre triple, the sixty-centimetre plank fence and then the eighty. If they cleared all five obstacles and felt confident then they could have a go at a very solid oxer, one metre high and about a metre and a half wide.

Jenny was feeling a little anxious. She had only jumped once, yesterday, and she was worried that she wouldn't be able to handle this.

Sofia strode into the centre of the field with Allegra at her side, brandishing a clipboard and pen.

"All right each of you over the three forty-centimeters first," she said. "Then continue on over the higher jumps. If you're all clear then you can have a go at the oxer, if you like."

Nick went first. They cleared the three jumps in Bob's usual workman-like style, nothing flashy, and then over the forty, the sixty and the eighty, without a problem.

"Shall I go on to the oxer?" called Nick, circling around the solid jump.

"Yes," said Sofia.

Bob cleared it, stretching out his short thick neck with Nick well forward to make it easier for him. Dom on the pretty Guinevere was next. They were all flourishes and flounces but a little careless on the eighty-centimetre knocking the top rail which came down.

"Okay," said Sofia. "That's enough, just go and wait over there." She realised this wasn't going to be straightforward. Obviously, Dom had jumped a metre before but he was careless and didn't get the best out of the mare.

"Right Maddie next on Cinnie," called Sofia. She stood watching and she could see that the brown mare just wasn't quite right, she wasn't exactly lame but she was uneven. Maddie circled her and pulled up.

"I don't think I can jump her," she called her face filled with concern.

"No, you're right, she's a bit sore," said Sofia. "Go and tie her up and we'll have a look at her afterwards. You can come and help me if you like."

Tom jumped next on little Goldie. His face was set with determination. He rode at the jumps as if it was a Grand Prix competition, and cleared every one of them, including the metre-high oxer.

"Wow! That was good!" shouted Sofia, thinking that the pony probably wasn't going to be able to go much higher.

"He is certainly a game, determined little rider," said Sofia to Maddie. "I think he is very promising, but he definitely needs a bigger pony. That little mare is brilliant but she is too small for him." She was more inclined to think well of him when she was going to make at least a thousand pounds profit by selling him Treacle.

Essie and Xanthe were hanging back, neither of them was keen. Jenny cantered a large circle with Beau, organising herself making sure she was sitting right. She pointed him at the three small jumps and he popped over perfectly, and she managed to stay with him, then she turned him for the fifty-centimetre and again they managed well, just one more, she thought and they went over the sixty-centimetre. This time she lost a stirrup and they were going too fast but she managed

157

to pull up, breathless and red-faced. She couldn't believe that she had just done this. She decided that she wouldn't try the eighty-centimetre, she just wasn't experienced enough yet, and Beau was rather keen, she couldn't just leave it to him.

"Oh well done Jenny! You're coming on so well!" shouted Maddie, knowing how hard the young girl was trying.

Izzie did a good round on Del who, as usual, behaved like a perfect gentleman. He understood that Izzie was nervous and he made sure to look after her.

"Don't bother about the oxer if you don't want to!" called Sofia. "You're both doing well." Izzie looked painfully relieved, she really did not enjoy jumping even though she knew that Del was more than capable.

Zane rode a circle on Himself. The little gelding was snorting, as if he were still a stallion, he was obviously a handful. But Zane wrapped his long thin legs around him and stayed in control.

"I'm just going to try the lower jumps!" called Zane.

"He's scared!" said Xanthe scornfully.

"No, he's not, that pony is really hard to ride!" said Jenny indignantly.

Zane managed to get Himself to leap over the three lowest jumps. The pony zig-zagged from side to side, trying to evade control and he cat-jumped with all four legs off the ground landing with a horrible jarring motion. Zane stayed on and then pulled him back to a walk, stroking him calmly down the neck.

"Yes, you're quite right, I think that's all he needs for now. He might be better jumping into the stream, something more natural perhaps?" called Sofia, although she wasn't sure that Himself was ever going to really co-operate with any rider.

"Come on Xanthe! Show us all how it's done!" She couldn't help taunting the horrid girl.

Xanthe pulled Gemstone into a very tight circle. Their canter was painfully jerky, obviously a very bad imitation of collection.

"How high have you actually jumped her?" asked Sofia.

"I've been training her for a few weeks now, but she's not used to these types of jumps," replied Xanthe snootily. She turned her to the smallest jumps. The mare looked very uneasy, she was flicking her ears back and forth and swishing her tail. Xanthe turned her in an even smaller circle and just giving her two strides to straighten up before the jump gave her a huge kick at the same time tightening the rein. The poor mare bounded over the forty-centimetre jumps, then without bothering with the fifty or sixty-centimetre Xanthe turned her for the oxer.

"Oh no," murmured Sofia feeling the need to put her hands over her eyes. Gemstone was looking wild-eyed and more stiff and jerky by the minute. She took off too close and tried valiantly to stretch over but Xanthe's reins were very tight and she couldn't make it. She landed on the back bar which broke and the poor mare staggered to her knees. Xanthe fell forward over her head and lay motionless on the ground.

Sofia bounded over bent over her. "Are you all right?" she asked anxiously.

"I've wrenched my neck, you stupid woman!" said Xanthe slowly. Sofia turned to the mare and saw that the broken pole had cut her around the hock.

"I think we might want to get the vet out to dress that wound," she said, thinking about insurance and liability, of all the pony club members to come a cropper it had to be this one!

"I'll ring Mummy and she'll organise it. I told you she wasn't used to jumping these tin-pot little jumps. That pole was too thin, that's why it broke!"

Sofia turned away, there was no arguing with such a ridiculous girl.

159

Maddie was slowly leading Gemstone up to the stables. Essie had jumped off Boxer and was bending over Xanthe, whispering to her.

"Oh, for goodness sake!" said Sofia. "Get up Xanthe and go up to the house. You can use Vanda's phone, ring your mother, ring the vet, perhaps you'd like the Air Ambulance to come and pick you up!"

Xanthe shot her a poisonous glance and slowly started hobbling towards the gate, making a big show of it.

"Right now, one of you take Boxer over and tie him up at the hitching rail and let's get on with this afternoon's schedule," said Sofia thankful that the hapless Essie wasn't going to have to attempt the course. She wondered whether she had the courage to make them do the water jump, she hated to think of more accidents. Then she had a brain wave.

"All right, we're going to try something different now," she announced. "We're going to practise some cross-country techniques in the schooling field. Some of you hold the ponies while the rest come and help me arrange some things. We're going to use just very small jumps and try some different lines, jumping fences off a turn."

Dom and Zane held the ponies while the other pony club members got ready to arrange the equipment. They were all looking a little mystified as to how one could practise cross-country in an arena.

"Jenny, you and Tom go over and get those old bending poles, you know the plastic poles that are embedded in pots of cement, we'll use them as flags."

"Nick, I want you and Izzie to set up some corner fences, like arrowheads, just forty-centimetres high but we want them at awkward distances from each other, say three and a half strides, that's about fourteen big steps. Then we'll put the bending pole here, so it's a turn, then two short strides over the first then change the line and perhaps four short strides or three long strides to the next one. Now as soon as it's arranged, I want you all to start cantering around and thinking about different types of canters. This is really fine-tuning the way that you control your horse, think about it as if you are changing gears. I want short uphill canters. Use half-halts to ask for more collection. Now uphill canters, shorten your reins a little and a bit more leg for impulsion. You have to have the feeling that the horse is in front of you, that you're riding from behind."

The pony club members did their best. They were all feeling quite serious after seeing Gemstone and Xanthe crash through the oxer.

"Now, first Nick!" called Sofia. "Keep the canter upright, full of energy, but quite short striding. Now around the corner and aim slightly for the narrow end of the jump and judge the take off as if there was a centre line through the arrowhead."

Nick did his best. Bob looked a little put out with this pernickety type of exercise, it wasn't exactly jumping hedges or stone walls like they did on the farm but he had a naturally short stride so it wasn't too difficult to at least produce a semblance of an uphill canter.

"Not bad at all!" called Sofia, thinking if they could just get through the weekend without anyone else falling off, she could relax. It was odd, it was as if she was losing her nerve and she wasn't even riding.

"Now who is next, perhaps Zane you might just want to jump the first and the second without the sharp turn. Just get him going nicely, a balanced canter and he can pop over one, then the other. That's good! It's probably what he needs, very low jumps so he can get his confidence."

"Jenny you're on a very experienced pony so I want you to turn around that pole and try and keep your balance."

Beau was a star and this time Jenny felt like she had a measure of control. She wasn't just a passenger.

"Izzie, again you're on an experienced horse, tighten up those reins a little and more energy. Try and look as if you're enjoying it!" Del managed it beautifully without much help from Izzie, who had pinned an unconvincing smile on her face.

"Tom you're on a very nippy little pony, this should be a breeze for you," predicted Sofia. And she was right, they flew it, looking as if it wasn't challenging enough. "If you had been on a bigger, more unbalanced horse, that wouldn't have been quite so easy," said Sofia.

"Dom, you're really going to have to do some work here, make sure that you accurately place the pony in front of the jump. I want more energy and less flourishing from the pair of you."

She was pleased to see that Dom was trying, perhaps he didn't like his younger brother to be doing so much better than himself.

"I think that will do, we'll go down to the stream and see how you go. I hope my nerves can stand it," said Sofia, looking up at the farm house, half-expecting Xanthe's mother to come screeching down like an avenging angel. At least Vanda was up there, she could exercise her tact and common sense.

They rode out of the gate in single file and made their way up the stream path.

"Now you know exactly what this is going to entail, seeing as how you built it. We'll all jump across one after the other, a bit like you're in the hunting field. Hopefully the ponies not so willing to jump into water with follow the lead of the others. So, I want Del first, then Bob then Beau, Guinevere, Goldie and last of all Himself. Then, if you all make it across, come back in the same order and we'll call it a day."

It was still hot so the thought of jumping into the water was not so bad. Del jumped perfectly as if he'd been doing cross-country all his life, which he had. Then Bob ridden by a very determined Nick who didn't want to be shown up. Jenny on Beau was thinking that if she fell off at least a dunking in the cool water wouldn't be that bad. It was almost as if she willed it. Beau jumped in with a huge leap and she felt herself jumped right out of the saddle and splashed into the water. The other pony club members started laughing when they saw her struggle to her feet, soaking wet. Beau had leapt up the bank and over the second jump. Now he stopped and looked around at Jenny as if to say, 'what happened to you?'

Sofia laughed with relief that there had been another accident but with no serious injuries. Dom had been about to jump but pulled away so they didn't land in the water on top of Jenny, who struggled up the far bank and caught hold of Beau's reins. Then Dom jumped in. Guinevere stopped dead in the water and put her head down for a drink and he fell off, and everyone laughed again. Dom was playing to the audience, and he took a bow. At least the happy mood had been restored.

Tom and Goldie waited for the other two. Dom managed to scramble on Guinevere while she was standing in the water and with a huge kick the grey mare leapt up the bank and over the jump. Tom and Goldie did it perfectly and then Zane pushed Himself off. It was the first time that day that the bay gelding looked happy, he splashed into the water and then with a great leap bounded out and over the second jump.

"Oh well done Zane, I know he is not an easy ride!" exclaimed Sofia. "Now everyone jump back and then we'll finish riding for the day." She was keeping her fingers crossed that no-one else would fall off.

"Now back to camp, those who need dry clothes get changed. I want the ponies unsaddled, rubbed down, watered and fed and then they can all go out in the field." She saw that the vet had arrived and hurried up to make sure that Gemstone wasn't seriously injured. The vet had put a bandage on her hock, but she was standing there with her head down, looking dejected and defeated. Xanthe was inside and Vanda was holding the mare while she received her treatment.

"Is Xanthe all right?" asked Sofia.

"She'll live," said Vanda curtly. "Her mother is arriving soon and is going to take them both away."

"Well there's always a silver cloud!" said Sofia mischievously. Then she had an idea, "I don't suppose while you're here you could have a quick look at another mare? I'll get Maddie to bring Cinnie up."

Gemstone was put in the stable and Maddie trotted up Cinnie. The vet rang his hand down the mare's legs.

"She's been having trouble for some time, I guess," he said.

"Yes," admitted Maddie. "I hose down her legs, I've got her on glucosamine and try to keep her off hard ground."

"I think it might be time to retire her you know," said the vet quietly.

"I guess you're right," said Maddie, tears in her eyes.

"If that's all I'd better get going. I'll ring up Xanthe's mother tonight about the palomino mare but she should recover well," said the vet.

Maddie led Cinnie away. She knew that she could always ride Max's horses but it just wasn't the same as having her own.

"Well that's been an eventful afternoon," said Sofia to Vanda. "Let's get these kids fed and they can entertain themselves tonight. Sit around and tell each other ghost stories, or whatever it is that one does at camp on Saturday night. I'm exhausted. I'm going in to shower."

"I'll get some of them up to help, I've set up the trestles on the terrace," said Vanda.

They were about to sit down to a most sumptuous meal when Mr Tregonning drove in. Tom raced out to meet him, talking fast.

"She is absolutely the best, just like Goldie but bigger, I know you're going to love her Dad." He led the way down to the small field and Sofia, about to start her meal, got up to go down with them.

Jenny sat there feeling as if her world was crumbling around her. She couldn't eat a mouthful. A leaden chill settled in her stomach, her prospects were zero. She felt unutterably depressed. Her usual sunny mood had blown away in the summer breeze and was never coming back. She felt as if she was being punished for her guilty secret – riding Treacle without permission. Only Vanda noticed her despair, but she didn't say anything. She had seen the way that Jenny had been with the little mare, the way she had lavished attention on her, sneaking in extra handfuls of feed and treats. It was going to hit her hard, losing her, and of course Sofia was utterly oblivious. Her cousin could be very careless of the feelings of others sometimes.

Chapter Twenty-Two

On Sunday morning, a cool breeze was whistling up the valley from the sea. Jenny woke with a heavy heart. It seemed that they'd agreed that Tom was to have Treacle. She tried to be sensible. At least it was a good home for the mare, but she had so hoped that Treacle might have been hers. If only, ... but then she would never have a £1000 and anyway she had nowhere to keep her. If only, by a miracle, Tom should change his mind, decide that he didn't want her, then perhaps there was still a chance.

Up at the house Sofia woke feeling rather virtuous. She'd put herself out and done the 'right thing' as Henrietta would put it, and her reward was over a thousand pounds in profit for the sale of Treacle. It had all been so easy, perhaps she should skip college and become a horse dealer. She remembered seeing a woman on Facebook who drove around in her truck picking up unwanted horses at very cheap prices, fixing them up and advertising them. But then she doubted that Henrietta would think that a respectable occupation for a young woman. Perhaps a side line during the holidays. She could go around the sales. Sarah could train and produce the horses and she could sell them to the students at college. She did feel rather smug, nothing could be easier!

She flung back the covers. Just one more day of this camp, and then she'd be back in Hampshire getting ready for college. Life was not so bad after all. Best of all was Rimmi waiting in the stable at Estrella, and he was the most promising prospect she'd ever had. In her bones, she felt he was going to be better than Gully.

The pony clubbers stumbled out of their tents and drank the hot cups of tea that Zane had prepared for them. Jenny stayed in bed with the sleeping bag pulled over her head, pretending to be asleep. When she did finally emerge through the tent flap she looked across and saw that Tom was riding Treacle in the field. The little mare looked brilliant. There was something so special about her, flashing gold in the early sunlight. Tom was jumping her over the forty-centimetre jumps and then he took her over the fifty-centimetre. Jenny felt the tears welling up in her eyes, she just couldn't bear it.

Nick called the pony clubbers together to go and catch the ponies and give them their morning feeds. Then they sat around the fireplace munching on toast and bacon.

"Absolutely delicious!" said Maddie. "It seems to taste so much better cooked over a campfire and eaten outdoors." She was determined to be cheerful even though she felt as if she was dying inside. The vet's advice yesterday had been the death knell, she could no longer pretend to herself that Cinnie was ever going to get better.

"I agree," said Essie, who was feeling rather lost, now that Xanthe and Gemstone had gone. She wished she hadn't been so horrid to Jenny, it was a bit embarrassing to try and be her friend again.

"So, it's the show jumping competition this morning," said Nick. "Sofia said yesterday that she was going to design the course and we're to help set it up. Apparently, they're bringing some of the jumps over from Penmar Hall."

"Sounds good to me," said Dom, thinking that he might just manage to slope off when the setting up was happening. They all looked up and saw Xanthe marching down to the field in her long electric-blue boots, a smug smile across her face.

"Oh Xanthe, how are you feeling?" asked Essie.

"I'm just fine and I'll be riding Beau today, at least he should do well in the jumping with an experienced rider like myself."

Jenny looked at her in surprise, almost disbelief. Surely if that was true then Sofia or Allegra would have told her. Xanthe was smiling at her with unabashed triumphant malice, it must be true.

"I thought Jenny was riding Beau," said Zane, speaking up for his friend.

166

"Well it's all arranged Daddy rang Tristan last night and they've agreed." Xanthe relished the idea that her father was on first name terms with Tristan Littleton of Penmar Hall.

Jenny couldn't bear it another minute. Tom was still riding Treacle in the field and now she was to lose her mount for the day, and to Xanthe of all people. She wouldn't have minded so much if it was Maddie who deserved to ride such a wonderful pony. Poor Beau would be lucky to come out of it without injury after the display Xanthe had put on yesterday. Jenny put her head down and got up and walked slowly up to the farm house. Xanthe's mother was there, twirling her pearls in one hand and gesticulating with the other, shimmering nail polish flashing in the sunlight. Vanda and Sofia stood there listening to her. They were both looking grim.

"Yes, well my husband is probably buying some of the land at Penmar, for another development you know. Not those tacky ghastly council estate type houses, really good quality four or five bedroom with double garages."

"So that explains why they've agreed that your daughter ride Beau," said Sofia. "I'm ringing Allegra about this." She strode into the house and then silently Vanda followed her and shut the door firmly. Xanthe's mother was left talking to thin air. She shrugged her shoulders eloquently and got in the shiny car and reversed out of the yard. Jenny, unobserved at the corner of the barn, heard the tyres skidding on the gravel.

She stood there not sure what to do. She wanted to crawl into a dark corner and sob but she needed to keep herself together. It would be too humiliating to break down like a big cry-baby. Sofia's ringing tones could be heard through the open window.

"So, that boyfriend of yours has sold poor Jenny down the river and he's letting that ghastly Xanthe ride Beau. What about Izzie? Does she have a say? Or he's the Lord of the Manor and what he says goes. You lot are still living in the dark ages and when you get married you'll hand your trust fund over to him and he'll lose the lot! You'll be lucky if Beau survives after what she did to that unfortunate cow-hocked mare yesterday. Poor Beau sacrificed so

167

that Tristan can make some money to try and rescue his family pile that has been run into the ground for God knows how many generations. Oh yes, don't bother to bring those jumps over this morning if I see your piggin' two-faced money hungry boyfriend I'll gouge his nasty squinty eyes out!"

Jenny decided she would go and sit in the tack room. She had never heard Sofia in full flight before and somehow, she felt it was all her fault. If she could just pull herself together, at least go down and help with the jumps, save face, act like it didn't matter. But really, she was beyond caring what the others thought of her. In fact, it would look strange if she acted as if she didn't care. She just hoped that Beau would survive, she would hate to see him injured like Gemstone.

"It's not going to fix anything you know, shouting at poor Allegra, she must be mortified at what Tristan has done," said Vanda to her cousin. "You go down and start organising the jumping, I'm going to see what I can do to make this better, at least for Jenny. You know it's hard enough on her to be losing Treacle."

"I don't know what you're talking about, she never had Treacle," said Sofia in surprise.

"Oh, really Sofia! You just don't think do you! Perhaps you could put Maddie on Nat for the morning?"

Jenny cowered in the tack room. Sofia marched down to arrange the jumps. She called over to the pony clubbers to help her. She asked Nick to organise everyone and showed him the diagram she had drawn.

"Don't worry about these two jumps there, forget it, they were going to be brought over from Penmar but that isn't going to be happening now," she told him. She called over Maddie and told her that she was to ride Nat. If she went up to the stable, she could saddle him up with a jumping saddle. Then she asked where Jenny was, but no-one knew. Izzie sidled over to her.

168

"I'm so sorry Sofia I had no idea that Tristan was going to do this. I've just rung him and he even wanted us to lease Beau to them but I've told him absolutely not, never! He's my pony but now it's arranged. Apparently, it's important to clinch the land deal."

"It's not your fault Izzie, I know you wouldn't have done this, let's just hope Beau survives it!" said Sofia, not bothering to lower her voice.

Maddie went up to get Nat and she found Jenny sobbing in the tack room.

"Come on darling, it's not that bad, something will happen. It always does, look I've got Nat to ride and all Max Winter's young horses, even though my lovely Cinnie is broken down."

Jenny felt better then. There was always something around the corner but she rather felt that she had used up all her chances. She showed Maddie Nat's tack and helped her saddle up. At least she was still good for something. Maddie mounted and asked Jenny to open the gates for her, so she would have no excuse to stay skulking in the tack room.

"He feels rather like those horses I ride at Max Winters," she said, maintaining a flow of conversation to give Jenny a chance to pull herself together. Sofia had explained to her that he hadn't jumped much and if she just took him around the low jumps and then they could pull out when it became obvious that he wasn't ready for anything higher. It wasn't that he didn't have the scope, more that he didn't have the experience. Jenny had red eyes but bravely carried poles from here to there and everyone was very kind, except Essie and Xanthe who were gloating. They stood around not picking up a pole, and laughing and pointing at other people.

"Right, the first round will be at fifty centimetres and if you have a knock down or a refusal then you don't go on to the next round, so we're looking for accuracy. I want you each to walk the course and work out for yourself how many strides between each jump, taking into account the length of stride of your pony. It'll be a real competition so I'm not giving you any hints how to jump, although of course you can discuss it amongst yourselves."

It was a well-arranged course, logical and easy to remember. There were several jumps on the diagonal across the centre of the rectangular field, and the double and the treble were on each of the long sides. The start and the finish were in the centre and that's where Sofia would stand with Vanda beside her taking notes and helping her to observe. Although Vanda had not come down, she had disappeared somewhere.

"Jenny would you mind coming and writing notes to help me, so we can keep track of the scores!" called Sofia.

A small practice jump had been put up in the laneway, it was on a bit of a slope but it gave the pony clubbers a chance to warm up and get their confidence. Although over-confidence might have been more of an issue with Xanthe on Beau and Dom on Guinevere. Tom might have looked over-confident, but in fact he was just utterly determined.

The pony clubbers mounted. First, they rode down the stream path, trotted back up and then rode up and down the laneway and over the jump. It was all rather crowded and then Dom jumped up the hill, pulled up with a flourish, spun Guinevere around on her hocks and then jumped downhill, straight into the face of Essie who was riding at the jump with false bravado. Boxer was well aware of Essie's lack of confidence and this gave him the opportunity to run off to the side. Essie shrieked and lost both her stirrups.

"You stupid boy!" said Xanthe contemptuously. "Look what you've done to Boxer!"

Dom just smiled at her lazily and lounged away.

Sofia had drawn up a list for the order of jumping; Nick on Bob, Maddie on Nat, Izzie on Del, Dom on Guinevere, Xanthe on Beau, Essie on Boxer, Tom on Goldie and Zane on Himself. So, if Himself demolished the course they would be due to raise the jumps anyway.

"Right Nick you're first up, off you go," shouted Sofia. "Jenny don't forget to press the stopwatch on my phone. I don't know where Vanda has flounced off to."

But Nick didn't ride straight in. There seemed to be a moment suspended in time and everyone turned to look down to the path beside the stream. Vanda was cantering bareback up the path on a small cobby looking dun horse, no hat, her long blonde hair streaming out behind her.

"It's Fred!" said Jenny.

"Where did she get that horse from?" asked Sofia.

"It's Fred, he lives down the stream on the other side," said Jenny as if that explained everything.

"Come on Jenny!" shouted Vanda. "Get your skates on, you need to saddle this steed up, he's to be your horse for the day."

"I don't believe it," said Jenny in a whisper.

"Well really!" exclaimed Xanthe. "That looks like a moth-eaten old creature, should be just about up to Jenny's standard, what can you expect from a girl off the council estate."

"That's quite enough from you," retorted Sofia, "you've only got Beau because your father bribed Tristan Littleton, so shut your nasty little mouth!"

"You can't talk to me like that," said Xanthe with a pout.

"She just did!" said Zane. "You hateful ugly cow!"

Jenny was walking forward, as if to receive a benediction. Fred had come to her rescue. She had only learnt to jump two days ago and she'd never ridden him and he'd been hanging out in a field with no training, but it didn't matter. He had been her faithful friend and then she had forgotten him, now he had come to her rescue.

"Don't worry, we'll wait for you," said Sofia. "Go and get him saddled up and then do a proper warm up, you'll be after Zane anyway."

"I think I remember that pony, years ago, he used to belong to that girl who went up-country and became a professional showjumper," said Nick. But no-one was listening, it was time for the first round. The best and most ambitious of them wanted to win the cup, and even more than that they wanted to beat the hateful Xanthe.

Chapter Twenty-Three

Nick pulled himself together and cantered through the course in a circular shape, counting through the jumps from beginning to end, to make sure he didn't go wrong. Then he turned to go through the start and Vanda pressed the button on the phone stopwatch. They cantered briskly up to the very easy cross-bar just three strides from the start then in a wide arc to the right to go down the long side, over the first element of the double, three strides and the second element. He turned right at the end of the field, three strides and he was over the hanging flat plank. Bob rapped it with his hind hoofs and it swung, but didn't fall.

"For some reason people always seem to hit those types of jumps," said Maddie.

Everyone was watching carefully, determined to learn from Nick's mistakes. He turned sharp right and back through the centre, over the easy brush jump and then did a long slow curving turn to the left and back down the other long side. This was the oxer, only fifty centimetres but eighty centimetres across. Then he gathered up Bob and did his best to produce an 'uphill canter' bounced towards the treble. The first element, one stride, the second, and then two strides to the third. He turned in a sharper curve to the left back through on the diagonal, over the single pole and through the finish.

"And a clear round for Nick on Bob," shouted Sofia. "Next is Maddie on Estrella's Nathaniel, home-bred and not long broken in but showing a great deal of promise."

Maddie rode in two circles before she set off, not exactly showing the jumps to Nat but letting him get used to the arena. He was usually so sensible but the competitive excitement had touched him and he shook his head and cantered sideways.

"Come on big chap, you can do this easily, tiny little jumps," crooned Maddie to him. He took confidence from her and he jumped a good round, just swinging from side to side on the approach as if a little

173

uncertain, but she managed to straighten him. He was so tall he could have almost stepped over the jumps.

"I think he'll go much better when the jumps get bigger, as he goes along," said Sofia. "But of course, not too high today, this is a perfect little event for his first competition."

"Maddie is a magic rider," said Vanda, who usually didn't even seem to notice such things.

"Yes, and such a nice person as well. It seems a shame to waste her on the likes of Max, I wonder if Henrietta would consider employing her. Sarah could take her under her wing and she would be good with the young horses."

"Yes, they can all be trained up and then you get to compete on them," said Vanda, perhaps a little cynically. Sofia grinned at her. "Actually, I believe she is a very good student, and aiming to study veterinary science at university."

"All right Izzie, I'm sure Del is going to find this very easy." And he did a copybook round, despite Izzie's somewhat uncertain aids.

"Her heart is just not in it," said Sofia.

"Thank goodness we're not all as competitive as you," muttered Vanda.

"Dom on Guinevere," announced Sofia.

Dom didn't seem to have listened to a word of advice and with much flouncing and flourishing he dashed around the course, lounging in the saddle, cutting corners and just managed a clear round.

"I doubt if he'll get around clear next time," muttered Sofia.

"Xanthe on Beau," she said. Xanthe rode in a circle twice, in exactly the same style of riding that she had used on the hapless Gemstone. Her reins were too tight and she used too much leg, also slapping the riding whip on the handsome little chestnut's shoulder.

"Oh, she is awful," groaned Sofia.

"Look there's Jenny on Fred," said Vanda looking over at the laneway. Jenny had ridden him down the stream path sedately at a walk, then trotted and cantered back up. The old dun pony felt very, very reliable, not at all like Beau or Treacle. He was solid and bigger, but he certainly responded to her aids, it wasn't that he was unwilling to move, he just waited until she gave him the signal. She cantered him up the laneway and he popped over the practice jump. Jenny found him amazingly easy to sit to.

"Come on press the button, if Xanthe gets time faults we're definitely going to eliminate her," said Sofia.

Beau was clearly not happy. He had his head tucked into his chest and he was swishing his tail from side to side like an angry cat. His ears were flicking around.

"He doesn't like her," said Sofia. "Come on mate, just buck her off and we can all have a good laugh."

But Beau was too well-trained to do more than show his displeasure. He jumped around clear very professionally and neatly. Xanthe flashed a smile at everyone.

"Now that's how you do it!" she announced. Disgusted silence followed her remark.

"Essie on Boxer," said Sofia.

Essie rode in at the trot. She was rising awkwardly and Boxer's paces looked even rougher than usual.

"He could almost be lame," said Sofia, scrutinising the pair carefully. "You know I'm not sure he is absolutely sound."

"It could just be that he is not elegant and smooth," ventured Vanda.

"She's got no confidence, nor ability, and no taste in friends," said Sofia.

Essie was destined to be the first elimination. She managed to canter Boxer over the first easy diagonal jump but the she turned for the corner for the double she misjudged the distance and didn't give the

175

gelding enough room and he put his head in the air and ran out, nearly cantering into the boundary fence.

"Swing him around and try again, this time make sure he's straight," said Sofia, even though officially she wasn't meant to be giving them advice. But Boxer knew that Essie had no control and no real desire to jump and he put his head in the air and ran out again.

"I can't do this!" said Essie plaintively.

"Try and jump him over the first jump on your way out," said Sofia. Essie ignored her and just rode straight out.

"Right cross her name off the list," said Sofia.

"Tom and Goldie," she called out.

Tom rode in on little Goldie and she looked so small but they did a very good round, perhaps a little too fast as if they were already in a timed jump-off.

"That boy is one determined bundle of ambition," said Vanda.

"Zane and Himself," called Sofia.

Himself was snorting, he seemed to have reverted to his previous stallion character. Zane sat him quietly, his long thin legs wrapped around him.

"That's not a suitable jumping saddle," said Sofia, "it's a straight cut show saddle."

"I don't think it really matters," said Vanda. Sofia frowned, she didn't agree but she wasn't going to argue. Zane pushed the feisty little horse into a canter and headed straight for the first jump. Himself hadn't done much jumping but he knew what it was about, but he wasn't much interested. He went over the cross-bar and then turned sharp right and it was only Zane's skilful riding that got him over the first, then the second element of the double. Then as they came to the top end of the field, he tried to canter sideways back towards the other horses but somehow Zane straightened him over the flat plank, then round to the right and over the brush, which he seemed to like better.

Then left and Zane gave him plenty of rein over the oxer and they were heading back towards the other horses and miraculously cleared all three elements of the treble. Then Zane took up the rein and with very firm aids he turned him left and over the last jump and through the finish.

"Oh well done!" shouted Sofia. "He's not an easy ride is he Zane!"

Zane nodded acknowledgement of the compliment and rode out.

"Well done Zane!" shouted a few of the children who were all grateful they didn't have to ride the recalcitrant horse.

By now Jenny had gone over the practice jump a number of times. Fred went steadily, placed himself perfectly for take-off and cleared it in a very professional manner every single time.

"You remember the course?" asked Sofia, who knew that Jenny had not walked it. Jenny nodded. Her face was pale and she was very conscious that this was a great chance for her and it meant so much that she should do at least one clear round, just to prove that a village girl could do it!

She gathered up her reins and straightened her back and cantered a circle. Of all the ponies that she had ridden this summer Fred was the easiest. Berry had been a little rough in his paces with his straight shoulder, Treacle had been very springy with her long sloping pasterns and Beau had just been a little too energetic and seemed to jump twice as high as was necessary, but Fred felt comfortable, like an old armchair somehow.

She turned for the first jump and pushed a little with her legs but mainly just left it to him. He popped over and then when she signalled to turn right, he obligingly bent the right way as if he knew the course off by heart, over the first element, three perfect strides then over the second. Then they cantered down and Fred took no notice of the other horses and ponies which were gathered to watch this round, everyone curious to see how Jenny and this strange pony would go. He jumped the straight plank very carefully making sure to tuck his hoofs in and leave nothing to chance. Jenny then almost forgot where to go next and she blanked out for a moment.

"Turn right," shouted Zane, seeing that his friend was lost.

"You can't help her!" said Xanthe spitefully. "It's not fair!"

"Shut up you ugly cow!" said Tom, cheekily, like all the others, except Essie, he truly despised Xanthe.

Jenny turned right and Fred almost found the jump by himself. Then she managed to pull herself together round to the left, over the oxer and her reins were loose almost hanging in loops and she was holding onto the saddle with one hand but Fred stayed steady and she was ready when they came to the treble. They popped over the first, the second and the third perfectly.

"Turn left!" shouted half a dozen of the pony clubbers in unison. Jenny knew where she was going now, executed the turn perfectly over the easy final jump and through the finish.

There was a burst of clapping from everyone except Xanthe and Essie and a chorus of well dones! Jenny fell down on Fred's neck and gave him a big hug to hide her tears.

"Right now, everyone, a couple of you hold the ponies, the rest into the ring to put the jumps up. Essie you're out so you can be timekeeper now."

Essie looked mutinous but didn't have the courage to object. So Xanthe was going to be stuck in the crowd of pony clubbers with no friend at all.

"I'm going to retire Himself as he did so well," said Zane riding off to tie him up to the rail.

It was only ten centimetres higher and now they'd been round once it would be easier, and the ponies would have learnt the course as well. Nick and Bob went first and clear. Maddie had been in two minds whether she should jump but Sofia nodded at her encouragingly so she went ahead. This time Nat jumped with more confidence, but he rapped the third element of the triple. When they had finished Maddie patted him encouragingly. Zane ran in and put the pole up ready for the next rider. Izzie also had a pole down on the third element in the treble.

"That was totally my fault," she said, patting Del.

Dom outdid himself in carelessness. He knocked the flat plank, the second and third element of the treble and even the easy final jump.

Then it was Xanthe, even as thick-skinned and arrogant as she was, she could sense the dislike of all the pony clubbers, but this just made her more determined to win. She tightened up the reins and slapped Beau down the neck with the whip and again the gelding swished his tail and swivelled his ears but he did a clear round. Tom rode in determined to go clear again and he did. Then Jenny again. This time she felt more confident, she had watched all the other riders and remembered the course perfectly. She cantered a neat small circle in the ring then through the start and suddenly she felt filled with confidence. Fred was the perfect schoolmaster. It didn't matter if her aids were a little unco-ordinated or they approached from the wrong angle, he calmly did his job and cleared every jump. Again, the pony clubbers clapped and cheered.

For the seventy-centimetre there were four riders left; Nick, Xanthe, Tom, and Jenny. Nick thought about retiring as he was so much older, really an adult competing against these kids but then he decided that that would be unsporting so he went ahead. They all jumped clear and the fences went up again to eighty centimetres.

This was a bit more of a challenge. Sofia thought about changing the course a little as perhaps the ponies were getting stale. She scrutinised her plan and decided that they would take out the middle brush jump and the last jump. They would go over the cross-rails, turn right to the double, over the plank fence at the top end then continue down the long side jumping the treble from the others side, then the oxer, which she would widen considerably, and then turn and up through the finish.

"Ok, have you all got the new course in your mind, just be aware of the oxer, it is considerably wider and doing the treble the opposite way may confuse the ponies a little."

Nick went first and felt a humiliated when he had two fences down. Old Bob tipped the flat plank and it fell and then he didn't stretch out enough over the oxer and brought down the second rail with his hind feet. So much for retiring to let one of the kids win, he thought ruefully. Then it was Xanthe on Beau and this time she loosened her reins a little and stopped flapping the whip on his neck and he seemed to be a little less sour and he went clear again.

"That pony is far too good for her," said Sofia, disappointed that Xanthe would be through to the final round. "We're going to have do it on time in the next round and I think take one more fence out, considerably shorten up the course," she murmured to Vanda.

"Tom and Goldie," she called. Tom was ready and he went straight through the start, not bothering to circle first. They sped around at top speed and went clear. There was a burst of clapping from the watchers.

"I think he'll win if it's on time," said Vanda, "he was six seconds faster than Xanthe and a lot faster than Nick."

Jenny couldn't believe that she was through to this round, and it was seventy centimetres, much higher than she had ever jumped before. But for some strange reason she felt comfortable with Fred. She had carefully memorised the altered course and she, like Tom, cantered straight through the start. Miraculously they went clear, even when she lost a stirrup over the oxer and had to turn sharp right to go through the finish Fred slowed right down and circled wide so she could get her balance back.

"That pony is rather amazing, doesn't look much but can you see how clever he is!" said Sofia in surprise. She hadn't rated the old dun pony much, he wasn't flashy or sharp, and his legs were hairy like a little shire but he could certainly jump and look after his rider at the same time.

"Right now, the fences are going up to ninety centimetres and we'll change the course again and this time it is the quickest clear round wins the cup that has so kindly been donated by Estrella Stables," she announced. "Now it is going to get tricky here, you've got some decisions about cutting across at a very acute angle and jumping the treble with just a stride or two to take-off or taking the long way around the plank fence. You go over the cross-bar at one, the turn right over the double and then missing the plank fence at the far end it's the treble and then the oxer and we'll move the finish to just beyond the oxer."

"Wow, that is going to be hard to decide," said Nick, thinking if he was still in it, he would go the long way around the plank fence. Xanthe screwed up her piggy eyes but wouldn't let on how she would do it. Jenny had no idea which way to go, Tom was sure to cut across the middle and make a sharp turn into the treble with nippy little Goldie. She couldn't decide whether to take the long safe option, after all the fences were substantial now and it would take all her effort just to stay in the saddle. She was to go last so she would watch how the others did it.

Xanthe went first and she chose to go the long way but riding very fast. She flew through the start over the cross-rails then curved round to the right over the double then she went flat chat to the top of the field and curved into the treble clear and then clear over the oxer.

"That's a pretty fast time," said Vanda. "It's going to be hard to beat."

Tom took off at the fastest gallop he could manage through the start over the cross-rails then he turned with just a stride to spare before the double then he went hard right at an angle across the arena and turned with just a stride before the treble and he was too close and despite Goldie's brave attempt at a helicopter jump she pulled the first rail, then the second, and then the third. She pulled herself together and managed to get over the oxer but it was obviously an effort for her.

"Well he was a few seconds faster than Xanthe but with three jumps down it looks like the spoilt brat is going to win," said Vanda in a low voice.

"Oh Jenny, it's just too much to ask, to beat that time and go clear," said Sofia.

The pony clubbers had fallen silent. Xanthe was the last person any of them wanted to win but they could hardly expect Jenny and Fred, the outsiders, to beat her, much as they would have liked them to. But Fred thought differently. It was as if he knew the score, he watched the others. It was the jump off and he'd done this a hundred times before, in his younger days, and ponies are like elephants – they never forget. Jenny had decided that she was just going to be careful and go for an honourable second if she could, but it seemed that Fred had other ideas. She turned and they cantered smartly over the cross-rails and then right over the double and then she had planned to canter at a smart pace around the top of the field but Fred seemed to balance himself and almost pause and she thought, no we can try this, and they turned at an angle across the field but she aimed a bit further into the corner so there were two good strides to the treble. Fred bounced over each element, nowhere near touching them. Then Jenny leant forward a little and threw the reins at him. On any other horse, this would have been a mistake but not with Fred. He galloped the few strides and launched himself over the oxer with inches to spare and through the finish.

There was a burst of incredible applause from everyone but Xanthe and Essie.

"Jenny, you did it! You did it! You're amazing, I knew you would always be amazing!" said Sofia suddenly imagining that this was all down to her. Vanda smiled happily. It seemed that sometimes good did triumph over evil. She suddenly had a vision of Beatrice smiling down from heaven, she would have approved of this outcome!

"Two and a half seconds faster than Xanthe and Beau, you win Jenny and Fred!"

Jenny sat there the tears running down her face. She couldn't believe it, she had won the cup! It was like all her dreams and all the stories she had read rolled into one moment of exultation. The future stretched before her like a golden stream.

She rode forward and Xanthe had to come in and ungraciously accept the rosette for second and Tom took his cap off and gravely thanked Vanda for the third rosette. They did a lap of honour and Xanthe galloped past Jenny and took the lead but everyone was laughing at her. It made her look even more of a fool.

Jenny slid off and she felt her knees buckling. She had to sit down. Excitement entirely overcame her.

"Three cheers for Sofia and Vanda!" called out Nick, like head boy at school.

"Hip hip hooray!" they shouted at the top of their voices.

A gust of cold wind came up from the valley, it was nearly the end of summer and soon they would all be back at school. Reality began to seep back into Jenny's consciousness. It would all go back to the way it had been before the big chestnut mare, Clovelly, had arrived at Treloar.

"Jenny before you come down from your cloud, I have to tell you something. I've just purchased Fred from Penzance Riding School. I've bought him for you on the condition that he stays at Treloar and you don't sell him. And I'll pay his expenses. He's to be your pony!" said Vanda.

Jenny looked at her in disbelief. This was the magic ending she had so hoped for but hadn't happened. Fred who turned out to be the best jumper on the Cornish peninsula, who she had forgotten when the other ponies had come into her life. Then she really did cry tears of happiness. Finally, she had her own pony!

Vanda smiled. It was a fitting ending to the summer before she left. And with Jenny coming up to Treloar every day and writing her emails she would know how Dane was going, and perhaps she might just cut short her trip to Russia and come back before next summer. It seemed that anything was possible when one galloped across a Cornish summer.

THE END

Printed in Great Britain
by Amazon